LIES THE DIRT KEEPS

HEIDI CHRISTOPHER

and I imagined her staring blankly out of her office window at the lit buildings walling her in.

"I told you it was a family emergency." I glanced back at the gas pump. Still guzzling.

"You can't go home, Johnna!" Her tone startled me. She must have sensed I was uneasy, because I heard her let out a controlled breath and then, "What I mean is that you'll miss the art exhibit next week."

Fuck. "This is more important."

"It's your big moment, Johnna. You can't miss this. Besides, your family doesn't give a shit about you."

Who did she think she was talking about my family like she knew anything more than I didn't get along with Laurel. "I'm not going to argue about this with you. My sister is missing."

Her chair stopped spinning, the distinct sound of a screech as it slowed to a stop. "What do you mean?"

I could have sugar-coated it, but I blurted everything. "No one has seen her since Saturday and now her best friend has been found dead and—"

"Listen, Johnna. This sounds like something the police should handle. If another girl has been found dead, then they'll take Ori's case seriously and find her before you even get there. Has anyone called the police?"

I pushed the toe of my shoe into a tar bubble on the freshly paved gas station lot. "No. Laurel convinced me that Ori was just blowing off steam from a fight she had with her boyfriend, but Dahlia's death has me feeling like something terrible has happened." Asphalt spread around my shoe's sole, and I immediately regretted digging into the surface.

There was a pause, keys clacking away on her laptop. "Listen...turn around, come home. I'll get in touch with the authorities and keep you apprised of any—"

"I know I'll be missing my big chance, but this is my sister, and I have to find her."

Another pause and then, "You're making a mistake, Johnna."

The gas pumped clicked off. "I have to go." I hung up and slipped my phone back in my jeans, walked toward the store.

Rolling papers were on my list, along with a cold Cherry Coke and a bag of pizza combos. I set down my items on the counter, chewed my bottom lip while the clerk glanced me over.

"Someone's having a good time tonight." He raised his eyebrows in a playful way that made me uneasy, his plump cheeks flushed, an annoying perk in his voice.

I pulled my items toward me when my card beeped in the reader. "I don't need a bag." I walked out without a receipt or a "thank you" and felt like an asshole for not being able to make small talk with the guy, but when my anxiety had its teeth in my brain even eye contact was stressful.

Inside my car, I lit the roach from my previous joint. Chilling in the parking lot to roll a joint wasn't a good idea, especially with the cashier staring at me. I gave him a nod, let him know I saw him gawking, and drove back onto the highway.

The next hour passed in a blur of memories I kept trying to push back, my defensive pitchfork, rusty and missing prongs. I was halfway into North Carolina when my phone rang, Gabe's number spread across the screen. I had programmed it in after he called me the first time. Maybe Ori was back, and I could turn this bitch around.

"Did Ori come home?" I didn't mean to skip hello, but all I cared about was his answer.

He cleared his throat, "No, Johnna. I'm not calling about that."

No? "What's up then?"

a good impression on Rhel. If I remembered it right, I made a great impression, all the way to a secret summer fling and a lot of making out and roaming fingers.

I smiled at the memory, wanted to go back to that summer where it smelled like Marc Jacobs perfume and tingling lip gloss.

I turned right and headed for the heart of town, curiosity leading me. The Piggly Wiggly was closed for the night, which sucked because I wanted to pick up some tampons before checking into the motel. My period was due, and I wanted to be prepared for that at least...among all the things I couldn't possibly prepare for.

There was a new burger joint, lights still on but dimmed in the front dining area, a skinny high-school kid mopping the floors. Ornamental streetlights trailed off to ugly utility poles with fluorescents, sheet rain like needles in the ugly glow.

Tantrums, the local bar, was ahead, its big neon light cast like red glass across the wet road. I had my first line of coke in the men's bathroom with a guy I'd just met. I ran in there to pee because the ladies' was full, and there he was, tall, dark hair, dark eyes, a fucking chiseled masterpiece. We fucked in the back of his brand-new extended cab GMC truck out in the parking lot. He came; I didn't.

My hands gripped the wheel. A part of me wanted to stop in and get drunk. I could walk to the motel from there, rain or not, and at least I'd get through the awkward first night easier. But my head still throbbed from my cage match with the stairs, and I needed to take out my contacts. So, I looked back to the road and pressed the gas.

I got all of a foot down the street before I saw the fight on the corner of the bar parking lot, lightning cracking overhead. Two guys, both throwing clumsy punches, one off kilter much more than the other, but when a punch landed and the face it hit spun my direction, my breath hitched in my throat.

"Michael?"

Goddamnit.

CHAPTER FOUR

I flung my SUV into the lot, slammed the breaks, tires grinding the gravel underneath, and jumped out.

"Michael!" I ran over in time to hear his fist thud against Jamie Hager's jaw. His homey since they were kids. "What the fuck, guys? I thought y'all were friends!" My voice startled them, and they stumbled to stare at me, blinking. They'd attracted a crowd, and I knew half of them too. *Fucking great.*

"Johnna!" Jamie exclaimed. His voice was more surprise than excitement, and I couldn't place why that bothered me.

"Yo, Hollywood!" Some guy shouted from the crowd. I didn't know who.

"Don't you take pictures of dead shit?" another voice said.

"Johnna?" a smooth voice said from inside the crowd. Kimber Hager, Shannon's older brother, parted the human floodwaters like Moses. He was the last person I wanted to see. Men who hurt women for rejecting them were exactly the kind of men to stay clear of, and I had rejected Kimber several times.

"Why has the eldest Kern returned?" he asked, a fluctuation in his voice that teetered on nervousness. But a nervous Kimber wasn't the Kimber I knew. Something was up.

"You know that isn't my last name." I tried to keep things cordial.

His lips smacked. "Oh, that's right. You're LaGrange. River rat blood."

Kimber loved pushing people's buttons, but I was a contactless machine—hands free, no pushing. "Still charming as ever, Kimber." He sneered; my stomach shrank. "Why are you letting them fight?" I motioned to Michael and Jamie who hadn't figured it out yet that they were both finished. "What are they even fighting about?" I wiped drizzle from my eyes, the rain falling soft then.

Kimber stepped toward his little brother...put his hand on Jamie's shoulder to steady him. "Does Shannon know you're back in town?"

Fuck me. I hadn't decided for myself that I even wanted him to know. Could no one in this town keep their mouths shut? "Hopefully I won't be here long enough for him to find out."

Kimber laughed, deep and methodical. "Now you know better than that. Nothing stays quiet here. He already knows you're coming." He drew his hand and whacked Jamie across the face. "Wake up. We gotta go before the bouncers call the cops. We don't want our brother arresting us, now do we?"

Kimber was the kind of guy who was always one step ahead. Whenever we partied at places where there were no trespassing signs everywhere, he'd take them all down so the police couldn't charge us. "We can't know if there aren't signs posted," he'd say when the cops would come. So, I felt like I needed to keep my knowing Shannon was a police officer to myself. I didn't want Kimber knowing I'd searched Shannon on the internet. "He's a police officer?" I tried to sound convincing.

Kimber's eyes narrowed, a curiosity shining through. "He signed up the day after you left. But you knew that already."

Coy son-of-a-bitch. I hated that he knew I knew. "So how

does that work? A police officer with a felon brother?" Kimber's smug grin dropped to a flat line, and I was pleased with myself for knocking the coy right out of him. Kimber grabbed Jamie around the arm and pulled him toward his truck.

I looked over at Michael, his back against an old pickup I assumed was his, tongue pushing against the inside of his cheek. He spat, a red wad splattering on the gravel. "I'll take you home. We can come back for your truck tomorrow."

Michael's eyes squinted as he stared at me. "This piece of shit ain't mine." He popped his butt off the truck and walked over to me, his weight bearing down on my shoulder.

I scanned the lot. Most everyone had left already. "Where's your truck then?" I let him lean on me while we walked to the passenger side of my car.

A huff shot from his throat. "It's in the barn at home."

"Why?" I struggled to keep us upright. Michael was a big boy and was letting his body weight fall on me.

He locked a glass-eyed glare on me. "Doing some work on it." He exaggerated ducking his head to keep from smacking it on the door frame, and I tried not to get pissed at how drunk he was.

"Tell your dad hi for me," I shouted to Kimber, shutting the passenger door and walking around to my side. Their father was always nice to me. Shannon had told him about Barrett, so he went out of his way to invite me over to hang out on the pier and fight over who was riding the jet ski next.

Kimber ran his fingers through his wet, black hair. "I want what you're on." He winked, and goose flesh crawled across my neck. Kimber had always been a wild card, known for doing bad shit that was too bad even for me. Driving under the influence, trespassing to steal shrooms from cow fields, throwing parties in abandoned farmhouses, those were my boundaries then, stupid and reckless but still.

Kimber cooked drugs in old mobile homes he and Jamie hauled out into the woods.

I closed the door, wiped the inside buttons dry with napkins I had from the drive-thru I'd picked up earlier. "What were you and Jamie fighting about?"

"Sometimes you just can't forgive people for shit they done." Michael's forehead was pressed against the window, his breath fogging it up.

"Look at me." I reached for his chin and turned his face toward me. "That's going to be a nice shiner tomorrow."

"It's not the worst thing that's happened to me."

I couldn't possibly think of anything bad that could have happened to Michael that he didn't bring on himself. "Momma's not going to like you fighting with the Hager boys."

He turned back to the window, closed his eyes. "Momma don't want you here."

"Yeah, well I don't want to be here." I hit the gas and sped toward the back roads where hamburger joints and night club brawls fell to Sweetwater's dark swamps.

***

The SUV hit a hole in the dirt road that had washed out from all the rain.

Michael's bobbing head smacked the glass. "What the hell!" His raspy voice cracked.

"My bad. I didn't see the hole. The swamps are flooding out on the roads."

He perked up, gazed out the windshield. "Damn, Johnna. You shouldn't drive back out in this tonight."

I gripped the wheel tighter, treads slipping under the loose ground. "I think I'll be fine. I'll just drop you off and leave."

He huffed, a grin peeling his lips apart. "That's gonna go

over like a turd. It's one thing to come uninvited but to not even say hi. She'll give you shit until the day you die." His perky attitude faded: quick as it came, it was gone.

We pulled up to the house, the living room light on—like always—and he opened the door, his back to me. "You better come in."

The farmhouse loomed, weather beaten and unkempt. It was pretty once, but even then, it was like some kind of two-story haunt with dark eyes watching. The house knew I was there even if Laurel didn't. *Goddamnit, Ori. I wouldn't be here if it weren't for you.*

I leaned over. "Don't slam—"

A resounding thud bounced off the house when the passenger door slammed shut. "Asshole."

I followed through the horseshoe driveway that Laurel used to keep up with white gravel. After Barrett died—*after I killed him*—and the money ran out, that luxury dropped off.

Another pothole gripped my SUV, and for a moment, I thought I was stuck, but then...I was out and rolling down the hill into the long driveway that would take me back out to a paved road. I reached the one-car bridge and stopped, water gushing over it like some giant brown snake in chase. "Shit." Michael was right. I wasn't making it out of there tonight. I bit my bottom lip and gripped the steering wheel until I thought my knuckles would pop out. I had to turn back to the farmhouse.

Rainwater turned the driveway into a muddy slip-n-slide by the time I parked at the front porch. When my socks felt wet against my skin, I realized my shoes were completely submerged. I walked around to procure my overnight essentials then ran up the crooked stairs and knocked, holding the screen door tight behind me so the wind didn't take it. No one answered, so I turned the knob and let myself in. The door screamed shut and still, no one stirred.

Where was Laurel? Asleep maybe? It was still a little early for her to be in bed. She wasn't yet elderly, not like the parents of most people my age. We were only sixteen years apart.

The stairway stole my attention, and when I dragged my eyes up it, my little self was standing up there in Sailor Moon PJs staring back down at me. My heart hurt for that little girl. She never had the childhood she deserved.

It was the floorboard at the top landing that had given me away that night. As a kid, I knew it was there, but that night I'd drank too much water before bed and was making a mad dash for the bathroom. That fucking floorboard. I stared at it in the dark, the way I had my eyes locked on the floor when Barrett called up the stairs for me. The scrape of his calloused hand down my arm, the smell of cheap whiskey on his breath. *"You sure are pretty and so grown up."*

"If you're gonna stay here, I'm gonna need some rent. Water and electricity ain't cheap, ya know." Laurel crept up, her superhero ability even in drunk mode.

I blinked away the blur in my eyes and turned to her. "I'm getting a room at the motel in town, but the bridge is flooded. I just need to stay here tonight. I won't run up your utilities."

She scratched a fingernail on her scalp—black hair bleached all the way to the roots—and drew a cigarette up to her mouth with her other hand. She glanced at my belongings, one small suitcase and my purse, which was almost as big as a suitcase. "That girlfriend of yours too good to come home and meet your mom?" She sniffed and walked through one of the two doorways that led into the kitchen, reaching for an empty rocks glass on the table.

God knew I didn't want to have that conversation. "No,

Momma. We aren't together anymore." Part of me was happy that she even knew I had a girlfriend.

She disappeared behind the kitchen wall, the sound of ice clanking into her glass, cracking as warm liquor poured over it. "You aim too high there, Laurel? Big money girl get tired of educating a country bumpkin?"

Bitch. I bit my tongue, tasted iron. A verbal altercation wouldn't solve anything, not now, not with her drunk. And I needed a bed for the night. "I'm just going to go up to bed. I need to take out my contacts."

The stairs creaked as I walked up. Ones that didn't use to. But the fourth one had a crack in the middle and made a loud screech if you stepped on it, and I didn't even think about it before my foot was already landing on the stair above it, my survival mechanism kicking in even after all these years. Lightning cracked and the entire house shook, and when I looked up at the hall window, I saw someone moving past.

"Michael?" I whispered, not wanting to alert Laurel.

The shape moved closer, still too dark to make out any detail, so my mind made up the missing pieces. Barrett's pale-faced corpse flashed in my vision like a fluorescent about to go out. I blinked, rubbed my tired eyes, and went for a second look. I knew it wasn't Barrett; he was dead, and I didn't believe in haunts.

White light exploded in the hall as another bolt struck nearby, assuring me I was alone. Cautiously, I stepped toward Ori's bedroom door. Could she be in there? Hope was shrink-wrap, and I was under a hairdryer. When I opened her door the hinges whined, pressing a sharp noise against the walls. I expected to see her just as I had every time I'd gone in her room before. Ori was always there, curled up on her bed with her books or playing her latest favorite video game on the console gifted to her at Christmas, the years when money wasn't hard for Laurel and Barrett.

I walked to a floor lamp, slid my hand under the lampshade to pull the chain, the dingy beige shade tilting crooked when I bumped it with my knuckles. A gentle click and the room illuminated, a bed made with an old quilt from Grandma LaGrange, the smell of fabric softener blooming. Ori loved that quilt, which was why I left it for her when I dipped. She'd take better care of it than me anyway.

I walked to her long dresser, its big oval mirror reflecting my image. I didn't think I looked so weary, but reflections didn't lie. On her dresser was a jewelry box, various knickknacks that only a younger generation could understand, and a bottle of perfume. I picked up the pink bottle, lifted the pretty butterfly wing-shaped lid, and sprayed.

Screams, the shattering of glass, a high-pitched sound of rubber screeching along asphalt. The sounds wrecked my ears, and I slapped both hands over them, buckling under the nausea stirring in my belly, and just before I retched, the noises stopped. A whisper of something tragic left in their wake.

Alone in my sister's room...it was the first time I felt her absence. Surrounded by her smell and her belongings, the dried flower art prints above her headboard. She was a ghost, and I was an observer left to sort out what she'd left behind.

Stop thinking like that, Johnna. But I couldn't shake off the fear in Laurel's voice when she warned me not to come home, yet here I was...holed up in an old house with no locks, and two very drunk, extremely unhelpful housemates.

CHAPTER FIVE

The sun peeked above the horizon, smearing pink across the sky, and I said a *thank you Jesus* when I came to the bridge past the farmhouse drive, and it wasn't washed out. I couldn't take another minute in that house, and certainly not when Laurel woke up, which is why I left before she pried open her drunk eyelids. Laurel could keep her salty ass attitude to herself; I had shit to do. Like find my sister...God willing.

As I drove through town, the smell of a BBQ smoker wafted through my vents, so I lowered my window and inhaled the scent. That's when I noticed a tick tick tick from my tire. "Ugh," I whined. "Must have gotten a rock lodged in it from Laurel's driveway. I noticed a coffee shop and pulled in. I needed coffee anyway. I hopped out and rounded my SUV to the where I heard the rock and saw it immediately. "There you are, you little fucker." It chipped my nail when I plucked it out, so I ripped the jagged nail off, tossed it to the pavement, and headed into the coffee shop.

I scanned the patrons through the large storefront window, making sure I didn't recognize anyone, a daily menu elaborately drawn in pastel chalk markers on the glass telling me I could get a 20oz house brew for $0.99 if I purchased a $12.99 travel mug. I came here for coffee not a fucking souvenir. I had plenty of those in the form of psychological trauma. Can't buy that in a store!

"That'll be $1.06." The cashier placed the coffee down in front of me, her eyes bright and youthful, like I remembered Ori's being. I pulled out my debit card and pushed it in the machine, the door behind me chiming as someone new entered.

"Good morning, Ms. Webber," the cashier said cheerfully, throwing up a hand to wave. Instinctively, I turned to the woman behind me, immediately regretting it once I saw it was Shannon's mother. She'd divorced their dad when we were in middle school, remarried a guy working at the post office. I held on to a lot of memories, but her last name wasn't one of them, and there I was staring at her like she caught me stealing her purse.

My soul gridlocked, a desperate urge to run grated the muscles in my legs. Shannon's mom hadn't been happy with me last time we met. I couldn't imagine things had changed. I grabbed my coffee, dipped my head down and kept my face hidden until I was behind her.

"I didn't expect you to say hi, Miss LaGrange," she said, southern drawl dripping in sarcasm. "You left my son without so much as a goodbye, so why would you speak a word to me?"

I stared out the glass door into the parking lot, the coffee in my to-go cup lapping at the edges as my hand shook with anger. "I'm sorry, Teresa. I wasn't trying to be rude. I'm just a little wrapped up in family drama." For her to act like she gave a shit about Shannon was a fucking joke, but airing the past's drama in the local coffee shop wasn't on my list of fun things to do in Sweetwater. I swung open the door too hard and flinched when it bounced off its hinges back at me. Once I was inside my car, I didn't bother buckling my seatbelt before driving off.

The library parking lot was empty. I sipped on my coffee and tried to remember what the library used to look like before the revamp of green vinyl siding, black window shutters, and a purple door, but all I could remember was the little boy leaving the library and getting hit by a logging truck when he slipped his mother's hand. White and yellow flowers adorned every business and residential home in town for the next year. Months after, the mother moved away.

I thought Rhel's mother would have moved away after losing her daughter, a child she cared about, but I guess she was holding on to memories that might fade if she left. If I weren't too afraid to talk to her, I'd tell her how much Rhel still lived in my head ten years later and four states away.

While I waited for the early morning to reach a point where I wouldn't be rude for knocking on doors, I did some photo editing on my laptop and answered some work emails. But it was 8:50a.m. now, and I wanted to talk to Gabe. I drove to his house, knocked on his front door, then stepped back, suddenly nervous. I felt vulnerable. The old house was his after his dad died in a car wreck on the interstate, a major pileup involving a fuel tanker and lots of fire. Eleven people died that morning. Sweetwater was truly cursed.

Foot beats shuffled to the door. "Who is it?"

"It's Johnna."

The door cracked open, sleepy eyes peeking through. "I didn't know you were coming."

"I literally told you I would. Besides, did you think I was going to drive down here and not come talk to you?" I flipped the strap on my purse that was coiled on my neck, pinching my skin. It was barely 9a.m. and I was already sweating. "Can I come in?"

He looked me over. "Sure." The door opened and I stepped

inside, immediately realizing I was three miles from town in the back woods and if I screamed—

"Sorry about the mess. I've been busy with work and shit."

I started looking for signs of Ori, or a poorly cleaned crime scene or anything that might be a clue. The place was a shithole. Why would Ori want to stay here? A rattling followed by the unmistakable sound of an old window unit cutting on behind me. Sweet relief. God it was fucking hot out. A good enough reason to slum it. Ori hated the heat and always stayed with friends during the summer. Maybe Gabe was more like a friend than Ori let on. Ori also loved being spoiled, and Gabe didn't look like the kind of guy who could afford her. "So, where do you work?"

He wiped his sleepy eyes. "At the Pig. I'm a butcher."

A fucking butcher at Piggly Wiggly. I'm going to be murdered here. "Is that right?" I scanned the room for anything I could use as a weapon, clenching the pepper spray on my keychain. "Doesn't look too good for a butcher's girlfriend to go missing, if you get what I mean." *Why did I just say that?* I was nervous, and weird shit always came out of my mouth when I didn't know what to say.

"Man, fuck. Are you serious? How do you think I feel knowing I might have to call the cops?"

"Might? Shit, Gabe, she's been missing four days. There's no *might*." I watched him closely to see if he took me wanting to go to the police as a threat, but he stayed calm.

"You're right." He pushed an empty shipping box up against the wall with his bare foot. "Ori orders so much shit; I can't keep up with the recycling. She usually handles it."

He said "orders" like she's still alive. I was no detective, but I watched enough crime TV with Danae to know that people who talk like the person is still alive really believe they are. Then again, anyone watching those shows would know that, and I haven't been around this kid long enough to gauge his intelligence. Ori was smart and beautiful, and those kinds of girls liked to date ignorant assholes. I dated my fair share: of course I was nowhere near as smart as Ori.

"So, what happened the night you last saw her?"

He scratched his head like he was trying to scratch away the grogginess of just waking. "I was a little drunk; she'd just come home, and it was late."

I flipped through my mental rolodex of questions. "How late?"

He snatched a crushed pack of cigarettes from the box speaker hooked up to his TV. "Midnight."

That's not late. Not in my book. Coming home late meant the sun was coming up. "Was she drunk?"

He shook his head. "Nah, I don't think she's ever drank, like ever."

"Another one escapes the family curse." Good job, Ori.

"But she was definitely on something."

Well, shit. "What? Like weed?"

He laughed. "That's not being on something...that's just smoking green."

I agreed. "Then what?"

"I don't know. Ecstasy, LSD, something like that. It was always something. She was into some weird shit, and I don't just mean drugs."

My faith in Ori's intelligence was fading. "What weird shit?"

He cringed, a snarl on his lips telling me it was a touchy subject. "That satanic shit. You know...animal blood and rituals in the woods."

I almost chuckled. "Uh-huh...so she was sacrificing animals to the dark lord?"

He flicked his cigarette in the air. "I guess. I don't fucking know."

"And you were mad at her for this?"

"No. It had nothing to do—" He stood up, face bent in anger. "Look, I don't know anything about that side of her, and I don't want to, so she never talked about it."

Ease up, Johnna. "So, what...she came home wired on something and you got pissed or...?"

He sat back down, lit another cigarette. "Yeah, something like that. She's too smart for all that bullshit. She's better than that."

Maybe he didn't know her very well either. "We can think that all we want, but she likes something about it. Any ideas?"

He took a drag, blew smoke rings like it was a trick I should be amazed by and shrugged. "I don't know."

This was going nowhere. "Come on, Gabe. Did things get physical? What was so bad about the fight that made her want to leave?"

His face went blank, pale. Another drag, this time longer, and then finally. "I told her to get the fuck out." He pushed the cigarette butt into an empty beer can. "And she did." A regretful laugh rolled up his throat.

"And she didn't say where she was going?" My peripheral picked up a dark spot on the wall in the next room. I looked more closely and saw it was a hole. "Who did that?" I pointed to the fist-sized spot next to the back door.

He shuffled another cigarette out, lit it. "Me," he said plainly, striking his lighter.

My filter abandoned me. "Did you hurt my sister, Gabe?" Like I said, I wasn't smart like Ori.

He stared me square, a long fucking pause. "Would I have called you if I did?"

I walked toward the door, wishing I'd kept the conversation

outside in the first place. But curiosity and all. "I don't know, Gabe, you tell me."

He stayed put, back against the kitchen door frame. "No, Johnna. I didn't hurt her. I love her." His chin trembled.

I pretended not to notice, opened the front door and said, "I hope that's true." When the door shut behind me a chill ran down my spine and kept its grip until I was safely back in civilization, the police station a relief until I remembered the half ounce bag of weed in my luggage. But there I was, the most I could do was take the roach out of my purse and stow it in my glove box.

I walked inside the station, my eyes darting in every direction looking for any sign of Shannon.

"Good morning," a monotoned woman said from behind a tall counter, hair pulled back in a ponytail so tight my temples started throbbing for her. Her badge was glaringly silver, *Sweetwater* blazoned in blue.

"Hi"—I scanned for her name tag—"Veronica." I tried not to chew my bottom lip. Danae said it made me look paranoid. "I'd like to report a missing person."

She stiffened; eyes widened. "We just had one, but—"

Acid climbed my throat.

"She was found dead. That girl looked for trouble everywhere. Guess it finally found her."

She was talking about Dahlia. "I'm praying Ori is just a runaway and will come back soon," I said, holding my breath the desk cop wouldn't say something stupid about my sister.

Veronica let out of sharp breath. "God, me too." She began typing on the computer and then stopped, brows creased in frustration. "Hold on, I need to get my supervisor. I'll be right back."

I sighed, relief and anxiety coiling inside my chest, two snakes trying to eat each other.

She was gone and back in a blink, and when I saw her supervisor, my throat locked up. "Hi, Shannon," I said, trying to maintain some sort of coherence while my nerves took target practice on my brain.

He smiled, not sweet like I remember but more of a courtesy. "Hi, Johnna. I was wondering if I'd see you."

I played it cool, though I was a little flattered he was thinking of me. "I guess Kimber gave you my salutations."

Confusion briefed his face but left in a hurry. "Uh no. I haven't seen him in a few days." He looked at the desk cop. "I've got this, you can go get lunch."

Her eyebrows drooped. "Don't you think I need to watch you go through this process with her? I'm still training." The way he stared at her blankly made me want to laugh and cringe at the same time. She tried to hold her ground, cheeks flushing.

"Fine," she said, defeated, and left in a huff that made her ponytail bounce.

"So, what can I help you with?" he asked.

"Ori's missing, Shannon. How do you not know this?"

He shook his head, aimlessly shuffled some desk items around. "Good question, since I saw Ms. Kern yesterday and she didn't mention it."

Yesterday? "What did you go out to the farmhouse for?"

He took a sip of coffee he'd been swishing around in its cup. "Your brother."

That was just perfect. "What'd he do this time?"

"I was following up on a case."

My mind buzzed with confusion. And then I remembered what I'd read online. "Are you talking about Dahlia Cochran?"

He nodded.

Shit. "Was it a homicide?" *And oh my God was Michael involved?*

His eyes darted away. "Johnna, I can't talk about this with you."

I tried to understand, but part of me felt betrayed he wouldn't confide in me. "What did Michael have to do with that?"

Shannon eyed me with an annoyed crease in his brow. "She was his girlfriend, Johnna."

Apparently, I didn't know shit, and it was embarrassing. "Oh, I didn't—"

"Johnna, why are you here?" he asked in a whispered huff.

I couldn't pretend his frustration didn't hurt my feelings. "I...I just...part of me hoped you'd be happy to see me."

His brows pinched together. "Johnna, I never wanted you to come back here again."

I was officially crushed. "I thought after ten years that...I don't know...maybe the pain of our break-up would have dulled."

He snapped a cautious glance at me. "So, you're here to file a missing persons report for Ori, right?"

"Yes."

He took out a pen and pad from his pocket. "Tell me everything you know." He clicked the pen to write.

I told him everything me and Gabe discussed, hoped he'd give me some indication as to the whether he felt Gabe was a suspect. "Laurel thinks that Ori ran off coz she's pissed at her boyfriend."

"So, Ori and Gabe got into a fight?" His pen hovered over the paper.

"I don't know. I just have a bad feeling, and no one else seems to care. Especially since I found out about Dahlia. I'm kind of freaking out, Shannon." God, I wished I hadn't unloaded on him like I had no control over myself.

He went to the desktop computer. "I care," he said, poking

at the keyboard. I watched him closely, reading every move he made, trying to determine if what happened between us ten years ago still weighed on him or if he was just being an asshole like his brother, Kimber. Maybe big brother had finally rubbed off on him. But as I watched, his eyes lit blue from the computer screen, I saw a man who'd grown into a life of gun belts and procedure. He seemed like a machine, emotions in check, even his movements seemed structured. I didn't know this Shannon, but I felt a little lighter knowing he was involved now. Like his knowing would make Ori magically appear. I wasn't surprised that he followed me to my SUV when we finished up, made a comment on how much he liked my vehicle.

"My ex bought it for me." I expected a sly comment about me stacking up the exes in my life, but he didn't say anything about it. Still a gentleman? Maybe he just didn't give a fuck.

"So, how's city life been treating you?" This wasn't a question to ask in passing. Not between two people with our history. He wasn't ready to let me go just yet, and I wasn't bothered.

"Better than this place did." I almost felt bad for talking shit about the town he served, but he knew my past.

"Well, I'm glad you found a place that makes you feel safe." He fidgeted with the sunglasses he'd pulled from his pocket but hadn't put on yet. I guess he felt as awkward as I did...having a giant wound between us and neither of us willing to bandage it. I didn't want to air things out, no matter that he might want to. It'd be like chewing an old piece of gum peeled from a handrail.

But I also didn't want to talk about me. "You got a girl, or are you keeping all the ladies around here on their toes?"

He let out a husky laugh. "There's a girl here I like."

CHAPTER SIX

There was a motel at the end of town, the southern end where things were more rural...if that were possible. I'd seen this motel a million times and had never been in it; not even when Barrett tried to take me there. Some big football thing was happening, and all the rooms had been booked. I remember sitting in the car waiting for him to come back. My stomach was sick, and I had to open the door to puke, all bile and yellow. It wasn't like he said why we were there, but I knew something was terribly wrong by the way he held his hand on my leg the whole drive over, smiling at me like a snake about to open its mouth.

And there I was now, waiting inside its lobby.

I smacked the bell on the motel counter, coffee wafting through the air as a fresh pot brewed from behind the desk.

"Hello?' I called out after waiting for the bell to summon someone.

"Coming," a shaky voice answered from behind a wood-paneled door.

I turned to look out the lobby window, rain starting to fall on the faded yellow Saturn parked out front. Aside from the 90s relic, there weren't any other cars there, which was odd since this was the cheapest motel in town.

"What can I help you with, miss?" the shaky voice asked from behind me.

I whirled around. A short, elderly man, thin hair combed to one side, collared shirt with a baggy sweater vest hanging off his small frame. "Hi. How much for a room?" I asked.

"Forty-three a night." He coughed, tucking a fist to his mouth.

I wasn't strapped for cash; I'd taken a stack of bills from mine and Danae's safe at her house. I wasn't sure when I'd be back, and half of that money was mine. "I'll take a room." I pulled out the wad of cash, and he cleared his throat.

"You should be more careful who you flash all that money to. An old man like me ain't no threat, but there are some unsavory folks staying here. You ought to be more careful."

He was right. I was being careless, but at that moment I didn't give a fuck. All I could think about was how tired I was and how finding Ori was still so far out of my reach. "Thank you," I said, hoping he was honest and would keep our interaction to himself.

"I give discounts on longer stays just so you know. If you want the week, I'll give it to you for two hundred."

I took a second to do the math. A week should cost about three hundred bucks. "That's a heck of a discount. How you making any money giving away your rooms like that?"

"I don't do it for everyone." His furry gray brow dipped, and he looked up at me, concerned. "But you don't seem like the normal deplorables that come through here. You look like you could use a life raft, if ya know what I mean."

I could have used that life raft fifteen year ago. "Well"—I count out enough to rent me a week—"Here you go."

He reached out, little wobbling fingers brushing over the

tops of my hands. He took the bills in his hand, licked a finger and started counting. I realized he was going to take a while, so I turned back to the window, catching a headline from the box TV mounted in the top corner above the door.

POLICE RULE THE DEATH OF HORRY COUNTY WOMAN A HOMICIDE.

I blinked, took a step closer. I almost asked for the clerk to turn it up, but then he'd get distracted from what number he was counting. A reporter started talking, an older woman with blonde hair and a red blazer. But the makeup and fancy suit didn't cover up the fact that she was all country. I wondered if she went to school with my folks. She seemed like she was from these parts, but I guessed anyone with a southern accent seemed like home.

"Twenty-three-year-old Dahlia Cochran was found dead and now police are ruling it a homicide. According to the sheriff's department, Dahlia Cochran was shot and then dumped in the swamps near the old Kern farm. Police are still searching for a suspect."

My body flushed, then went cold. My mind began putting pieces of a puzzle together that had no picture. Ori was missing and a girl was found murdered near the farmhouse and she was dating Michael, and there was nothing I could do except wait on my motel key.

"Did you know her?" The old man's voice snatched me away from the news.

"Uh, no. No, I don't, uh didn't...I didn't know her." My eyes flicked from the TV to the clerk. "Did *you?*" In small towns, people usually knew everyone.

"I've seen her around town before but that's about it. We don't run in the same circles if you get what I mean."

I couldn't help the laugh that bubbled up. He was a good sixty years older than Dahlia.

He reached behind him, lifting a key off the hook board. "Here you go. Room seven." He pointed out to the parking lot. "Go around back; it's on the last row. I ain't got nobody in those rooms, so if you're careful, you can keep from running into folks here at the motel."

I took the key, offered a smile and scanned the parking lot again before heading out.

My key tag room number was almost peeled completely off, but the dirt on the sticky outline of the number seven stood out. I opened the door, the smell of old cigarettes and dank AC greeting me. I put my bags on the small table under the window. Every motel was set up the same, two beds separated by a lamp stand and a round dining table with two chairs under the windows that shared a wall with the door. No wonder the owner hadn't updated anything, he was basically giving away the rooms.

My phone buzzed and a text banner flashed across the screen. *Danae.* She must have found out that I'd left. All I felt was an airplane on my chest and its turbine engines roaring in my ears. I threw a notebook on the table, sat down and lit that joint I'd been craving all day. I drew it in slow, letting the smoke fill my lungs, my nose, my head, and then blew it out toward the back of the room.

I took the pen in my hand and started writing things down about Ori's disappearance...everything I knew so far.

Then I thought about things that might have happened. What if her car broke down and a long-haul trucker kidnapped her...the trucker calling a friend with a towing service to tend to the car while they drove her to a secure location to be sex trafficked? Had she fallen for the lost kid that needed help finding their mom and then boom, she's in some guy's cellar being tortured? "Fuck, Johnna, that's horrible."

I blew out another plume of smoke. If anything like that were true, I'd never be able to live any kind of normal life ever again. It was one thing to traverse life with my own traumas, but to exist in a world where my sister was horribly murdered or, fuck...just never found...I don't know how I could manage that reality.

I dropped the pen, eyes darting over the words that meant bad things for Ori. My heart fluttered, a sign anxiety was bubbling, a flopping fish in my chest was how I described it to my doc who said *That's normal for anxiety*, but didn't tell me how to fix it, just threw a prescription at me and expected me to forget the night I'd found my best friend, Rhel, blue-faced, eyes blank, dead as the day was over.

For some reason, Rhel correlated to Ori in my mind, and I realized I needed to find out who her friends were. Shannon would do his investigating by the books, but I didn't have to, and I wanted to get to them before he did in case his inquiries scared them from speaking to me. I was writing a list of things I needed to do the next day when my meds kicked in and I drifted off to sleep.

Her blood tasted like a dirty penny, tangy and metallic in her mouth, and something strong and dark pulled her under the brackish swamp water. Something heavy pressed on her neck, her face grinding into the muddy bank.

I shot awake, nearly falling out of the chair. "Fuck." I grabbed my lips, the foul taste of swamp lingering on my tongue.

My phone buzzed, and I slapped around for it on the table full of my shit.

"Hello," I said, head groggy after startling awake from the

nightmare. I didn't look at who was calling because in that awful moment, I hoped like hell it was Ori. "Hello?"

"What've you been telling these folks around here about us?" Laurel snapped, her words slick and venomous.

"I only went to see Shannon. Gave him some—" It wouldn't be smart to tell her about the missing person report I filed.

"Well?" Her insistence was a potato peeler on my nerves.

"I gave him all the information that you and Michael told me."

A soft strike of a lighter, the singe of flame to the end of a cigarette, a crisp, sharp draw of nicotine. "Michael knows all of shit about anything. Why'd you bring him into it?"

Always at his defense. "Momma, I'm just trying to find Ori. Michael only told me the last time her saw her, just like you, just like her boyfriend."

"Did you go over to Gabe's place by yourself?" Her breath hitched, and then she exhaled, and I imagined a plume of smoke rising above her head and shaping into two horns.

"Yes." It was a bad idea that could have ended terribly, but I was still alive.

"He could have done God knows what with my daughter and you just went over there all Inspector Gadget and shit."

"I'm obviously okay."

Another quick drag and exhale. "Yeah, well he's dangerous. Next time you want to play hero you should at least let your mother know; it's the respectful thing to do."

I slapped a hand over my mouth to keep from laughing. Laurel was a belligerent drunk who practiced respect as much as she sought sobriety. "I won't go over there by myself again, Momma." I pulled out a THC vape pen and pulled until my eyeballs wanted to pop.

"What's Shannon say?"

I wondered when she would ask. "He filed a missing

persons report and said they'd look into it." There, I ripped off the Band-Aid.

The distinct sound of fingernails clicking, a faint huff under Laurel's breath. "Well, I don't want you making a mountain out of a molehill. She'll be home soon. It's a waste you drove all the way down here for this."

"She's not a waste of my time."

Laurel sniffed. "Why don't you come over for supper. I ordered takeout."

I'd rather be tied to a bed in Annie Wilkes' house. "I can't, Momma. I need to edit some photographs for work." She went silent and the air around me thickened, but I held my ground.

"It's just so quiet here without Ori and Michael's always working."

Again, I tried not to laugh. Michael was working alright. Working at putting liquor down like it was an Olympic sport. But I heard the quiver in her voice when she said Ori's name, and even if she didn't love me, I loved her, fucked up as that was. I let out a breath. "I'm on my way."

CHAPTER SEVEN

On my way to the farmhouse, I tuned the radio to a local station hoping to get an update on Dahlia's murder investigation. Her body had been found on Laurel's property and damnit if that didn't point the finger straight at Michael. Another surge of worry flooded through me. What if he *did* have something to do with her murder...or know who did? Or worse...had Ori been in the wrong place at the wrong time? It's reasonable to assume Ori could have witnessed Dahlia's murder and became a victim herself. Was Ori in the swamps behind the farmhouse, too?

Fear became a parasite, wormed its way deeper and deeper, and before I knew it, I was pulling into Tantrums. Maybe Michael was there. I couldn't tell from outside because Michael's truck was in the barn. But Kimber's truck was there, and that meant he would make a point to harass me if I went in.

I should leave. I wanted to leave, the scene would be a lot to deal with, I was already exhausted, and Laurel was waiting.

"Fuck it." I turned into the lot, pulled in next to Kimber's truck, black paint lit red by Tantrums' neon sign. I got out, stared at his truck, and fought the urge to drag my key along the quarter panel. But I was a big girl, and I did shit different now.

"ID." The muscled guy in a Tantrum's logo T-shirt said from behind the check-in counter, a poster of a local band advertised on a corkboard wall above him, the thud of music beyond the double doors pounding in my chest.

I slid my ID under the plexiglass, a new addition since I'd last been there. "Michael Kern in there?" If this guy had been working the door any length of time, he'd know who I was talking about.

"Not tonight." He flipped my ID up to the light then slid it back. "Eight-dollar cover."

Shit. I was already there though, and I knew there had to be someone inside that could tell me something about what's going on in this town. I yanked a ten from my purse, told him to keep the change and pushed through the doors, loud music and smoke machine stench hitting me square.

It was a strange feeling being in a nightclub alone, without Danae, to be truthful, but what made it worse was to be solo and empty-handed, so I ordered a Sprite and lime from the pretty bartender with hella curves and a southern accent that melted my cold, dead heart.

If I weren't absolutely sure she wasn't into me, I'd have given her my number. A week alone in this town could break me, but she would've helped make it tolerable. I turned to the crowd, the dance floor packed, Billie Eilish's "Bad Guy" blasting. I bobbed my head trying to loosen up, trying to convince myself it wasn't a dumb idea to have come inside when Laurel was waiting.

"Johnna Johnna Johnna," a voice called, smooth as honey on a hotplate. I hated it.

Kimber strolled up to me, a pool stick in one hand, a beer in the other.

"Kimber," I acknowledged, wishing I had just gone straight to Laurel's instead. I didn't know what I was thinking, but seeing Kimber, standing over me all Paul Bunyan and shit, made me feel like a rabbit under the farmer's tractor.

"I didn't expect to see you in here." He took a swig of beer, licked foam off his upper lip.

"I'm looking for Michael." My eyes flicked to a nearby waitress, the urge to flag her down and order a shot of tequila pulled my attention away for Kimber long enough for him to notice.

"So, is that the kind of chick you dig?" His eyes shifted to the waitress and back to me...he took another sip. "She's a bit slummy for you, ain't she?"

"Don't you have a game to get back to?" I pointed to the pool table behind him where a woman leaned on her pool stick, an expectant look on her face.

He cut a half smile at me. "Wouldn't want to keep the lady waiting." He sauntered over to her, snatched her up by the waist with one arm and kissed her like it'd be his last; it was kind of sweet, until he turned where he could see me, stared at me while he drove his tongue deeper, pulled the woman's pelvis against his.

Ugh. I turned around, saw Jamie, Shannon and Kimber's youngest brother, sitting at a long bar that faced the dance floor. I walked over, sitting on the empty stool beside him. "Hey." I sat my drink down on the bar and lazily stirred it.

"Hey," he said, barely acknowledging my presence.

"Any prospects?"

He turned to me, confusion on his face, eyes red-rimmed, nose puffy, recognizing me after that moment of assessment passed. "Oh, Johnna." He raked his palms on his jeans. "You aren't supposed to be here," he slurred.

"I don't want to be here," I said, searching every part of his body language. I had to figure out what happened before Ori went missing, some kind of timeline to direct me. I needed him to talk, so I kept the conversation casual. There were three empty shot glasses in front of him. "Whatcha drinkin'?"

His head bobbed, eyes on the shot glasses. "Cheap whiskey."

I raised my hand and flagged a nearby waitress. "Two shots of tequila." Jamie probably wouldn't like my choice of alcohol, but he didn't seem like the kind to turn down a free drink. Besides, I couldn't stand whiskey. I hated the shit. It reminded me of Barrett's breath.

The waitress smiled and nodded, took off for the bar, so I knew she'd be back soon. I focused again on Jamie. "How's the business doing?"

He looked at me, a glint of suspicion in his eyes. "What do you care about our shop?"

Guess he wasn't drunk as I thought. I shrugged. "I don't, Jamie. Just making small talk, I guess. It's been a while since I've seen you. I don't really know what to say."

He huffed. "Yeah whatever."

I was used to Kimber being an asshole, but Jamie? He was always nice. Drunk or high on drugs but nice either way.

"Here you go!" The waitress came up from behind, chipper voice, bubble gum perfume.

I gave her a twenty. "Keep it," I said, sliding a shot in front of Jamie on the bar.

"Thanks!" She swished her hips over to another customer.

"To the good old days." I held up my shot glass, and he took up the other.

The corners of his mouth sagged. "To the good old days," he slurred, then tossed the shot back.

I didn't know what to say next, but there was a reason he and Michael were fighting, and I had a feeling it wasn't good.

Michael mentioned their fight being about a girl. Did he mean Dahlia? Had Jamie hurt her? For all the things Jamie was, he wasn't a murderer. But as I flipped through my bad scenario rolodex, I landed on something drug related. What if Michael owed them money or stole drugs from them, or lost money or stole money—he'd probably be dead if that were the case—but something was fucking going on and Jamie was going to tell me. "So," I flicked my gaze to the dancing crowd. "What's going on with you and Michael?" I nudged him with my elbow. "Ya'll fussing over the same girl?" Kept it light.

"You called it." His lips puckered and he swigged his beer.

So, Jamie liked Dahlia? Not a good admission since she was just found murdered. I didn't want my pitstop to be useless, so I figured I'd ask. "Do you know who might have wanted to hurt Dahlia?"

He twisted his head, a pop in his neck. He reached inside his pant pocket and pulled out a vape, took a long hit. "What... are you a cop now? Bet Shannon will love your help."

Fuck. I don't want him to tell Shannon I'm asking questions about Dahlia. I really underestimated Jamie's alcohol tolerance.

Kimber pushed in between us, leaned his back against the bar, fingers laced together on his stomach, all cocky and fully calculated. "You two look cozy as a puppy in a gator's mouth."

I'd had enough of the Hager boys for one night. "I better get. Laurel's got takeout waiting." I stood to leave, and Kimber grabbed my arm.

"Next time you got questions, you come to me." He squeezed tighter, trying to make his fingers touch. "You being here is only making all of this worse for your brother."

I kept calm, eyes flitting around the club for the closest bouncer, saw one staring right at us. And when I saw that Kimber also noticed the bouncer, I yanked my arm away. "And here I thought you were happy to see me." I gave him an *eat shit* smile and left. When I got outside, it was dark, and I hated the idea of rolling up to the farmhouse at night.

My SUV idled in Laurel's driveway, windshield wipers gnashing at the sudden downpour. Deciding on whether or not to go inside was like tying a string to a loose tooth and making myself pull.

I pulled.

This wasn't a proper home with bedtimes and a family dog. It was a prison with an alcoholic warden.

"Momma?" I called, opening the door and walking in, shaking off the rain that started pouring as I pulled up the drive. All the windows were open, curtains blowing, memories of summer nights whipping through my mind. A familiar scent, a cool breeze across my skin. Had Ori come home? Showered and perfumed and ready to get back to her life? I took a moment to acclimate inside the foyer. The entry way seemed so expansive when I was a kid; now it felt like a cavern that squeezed in smaller and smaller. My eyes dragged up the dark staircase, stopped at the top banister railing near Ori's bedroom door. I knew she wasn't home, but my heart wouldn't listen to my brain.

I was already halfway up the stairs when Laurel's alcohol-flavored voice gripped my spine. "Took you long enough. Where you been?"

I turned back. Laurel was at the bottom banister with a whiskey glass in one hand and a cigarette in the other, hip cocked and a glare sharp as broken glass.

"I stopped in at Tantrums," I said, salty she'd had such a tone. "Is Ori home?" My chest fluttered.

She jerked her head back. "Why would you ask me that?"

What? "Are you asking why I would wonder if she's home?"

Her face cinched up in the center like the mouth of a pull-string bag. "No. Why did you go to the bar?" She pivoted.

My palm hovered over the worn railing as I walked back down. "I saw Kimber's truck and wanted to talk to him."

She squinted. "I don't see what business you could possibly have with that Hager boy."

He was hardly a boy. "Michael and Jamie were fighting in the parking lot last night. I wanted to know what was going on."

Laurel turned away laughing, bra strap hanging off one shoulder. "What? Is big sis gonna beat up her little brother's bullies?"

I stepped down and the floorboard creaked, and I saw Barrett's face all over again, the sweat over his upper lip, the knowing in his eyes that what he wanted to do was so very wrong. "I protected him my whole life; what's so different about now?" I knew she'd have something to say back.

"Hmph," she shrugged. "I hope you like cold Chinese food, coz the microwave ain't worked for months." She pulled out a chair from the kitchen table, its pastel yellow trim chipped and fading.

I sat across from her, eyeing the food, picking up a spring roll. It was cold when I bit into it but good enough that I grabbed a second. Laurel ate mostly liquor and Sprite, with an occasional bite of lo mein. "How's work?" Something off topic of family matters might help keep the vibe elevated.

"What work. I ain't worked in months." She slid back her chair and hopped up, reaching on top of the fridge for a new bottle of soda pop.

"What happened?" *Fuck, why did I ask that?*

"My hip hurts too bad. I can't wear them heels no more."

Huh? "I thought you worked at the Walmart Distribution Center."

She rolled her eyes. "You know I don't like those nine to five jobs. They're too restrictive. I feel like I'm suffocating."

Sounds like something Michael would say. He hadn't worked a normal job ever. "So, you were waitressing? Bartending?"

Momma laughed, all throaty and silk. "No, honey"—the kind of *honey* that meant bitch— "I was dancing. How was I supposed to pay for all this?" She gestured around to the house. I wasn't sure what *this* she was talking about since the farm had been lost years ago and the house was falling apart.

"I didn't know things were this bad. Why didn't you tell me?" I would have sent money for Ori, and made sure there was food in the house, but I didn't know.

She turned to me, smiled. "You made such an effort to leave us all behind. I didn't want to bother you with it." She sipped her drink, bit a piece of ice down and spat the other part back in. "Besides, Michael provided for us. He's always been there for me, and your sister. Maybe you should thank him next time you see him instead of going on about his squabble with an old friend."

My face flushed, and I was sure it was the color of the red star hanging over the kitchen curtain above the sink. I slid my chair back, flinched when it squealed against the hardwood, and stormed to the bathroom. Laurel couldn't lie as well as she thought. I knew Michael wasn't working, not anything legit. He was slinging drugs for the Hager brothers. I just knew it. But it'd do no good to argue with her; she'd only take his side. Even if she found out Michael's affiliations led to Ori's disappearance— which was totally plausible—she'd still baby him.

I slammed the bathroom door shut and jumped at the sound. The light over the mirror flickered, and I walked over to check the bulb, make sure it was screwed in all the way. My fingertips gently gripped it and turned it tight. "See, Laurel, I'm useful, too," I mumbled sarcastically. I turned on the cold-water faucet, let the cool water pool in my hands, splashed it over my face until the heat left my cheeks.

I reached for the hand towel, wiped my face, heard the light flicker again and looked up. There was a reflection in the mirror of someone standing behind me, the smell of creamed corn suffocating the wall plug-in air freshener. *Barrett?*

I spun around, heart racing, light flicking on and off, and there was nothing. Just me and the thudding in my ears and fuck that god-awful smell of something dead. For a second, I was frozen, awe pressing down on my shoulders. *What the hell, Johnna?* I hadn't smoked since the motel and weed didn't give me the hallucinations...my sleeping meds did, but I'd been off them since the night I sleepwalked down a flight of stairs. So, what then? Had someone slipped something in my drink at Tantrums? I straightened, stared forward, noting the room and how it absolutely was not spinning. My head was fine, my vision clear. I couldn't explain what I saw, only that I saw something and then it was gone.

I slung open the door, half expecting for whoever I saw to be standing on the other side...waiting. But there was nothing except me and that fucking staircase, a soft whoosh of air passing through the house from window to window. The storm outside had passed over already.

A pain crawled up my jaw, and I realized my teeth were clamped shut. I rubbed my eyes, patted my cheeks, and walked back to the empty kitchen, takeout left opened and strewn about the table. From the living room doorway I saw Laurel sitting in Barrett's old recliner, brown leather peeling away on the armrests, cat scratches on the edges. I didn't know they had a cat. We were never allowed to have inside pets.

Maybe Ori had convinced them. She had a soft spot for

animals, always feeding strays and building them little shelters in the woods just off the back of the house.

The television was on, a game show turned down so low I could only hear when a contestant hit the buzzer. "I'm going to head out now."

Laurel didn't look at me. "You should just stay here tonight. It ain't safe out there with a murderer on the loose, ya know?"

She didn't want me to stay; she was just being motherly, which made me ill. Too little too late in my opinion. "I'll be fine."

"Suit yourself. You always do." She picked up the remote and turned up the volume to where she couldn't hear me unless I shouted.

I was in the hall when Michael walked through the door, drenched, smelling like he took a swim in a pool of whiskey. He barely looked at me, gave a weak smile that felt forced, like one Laurel would give me. "See ya later," I said, hoping he'd stop and talk to me. There was never any making Michael do anything. He did what he wanted, and if that meant completely ignoring me, then that's exactly what he'd do.

And that's what he did.

I watched him skulk up the stairs, surprisingly measured considering his blood was more alcohol than not. "Nice talk." I shut the door behind me, minded the wet wooden porch stairs and got in my car. It was the first moment I was able to relax since I arrived there an hour ago. I let out an anxious breath, tried to bury the image I saw in Laurel's bathroom, the smell still lodged deep in my nose. I lit a joint, breathed it out through my nostrils just to kill the scent of death I'd smelled all those years ago. It did the job, and I put the SUV in drive, heat lightning fingering the sky as I passed through the wood-lined driveway.

CHAPTER EIGHT

I wanted nothing more than to cleanse the day away, as if somehow a shower would wash away the smell buried in my mind. I let hot water run down my back, watched it swirl down the drain like I had every time I showered after Barrett had raped me.

But no amount of washing could rinse that away. I tried. Filled a tub with boiling water once and plunged myself into it before I could talk myself out of it. I don't know how I escaped that with only mild burns. Laurel said—after she stopped yelling at me—that it was because I was a witch, and their flesh was strong. It wasn't meant to be a compliment. I never believed it anyway, but then again, I never thought a grown man would hurt me and that my momma would call me a liar when I told her.

I hadn't changed out of the towel I'd wrapped around me and was lying on the bed clicking through photos I'd taken of Danae on my new couch. I'd invited her over to my apartment to discuss the process of me giving back the SUV and a stack of books I'd mistakenly taken when I'd moved out. I thought our talk went well...that we agreed the split was amicable.

I laid the camera down on the bed next to me, stared at the ceiling, gold fleck glinting off the lamp light. I began to count them, a great distraction for the shit-pudding memories were serving, when my phone rang, Danae's beautiful face lighting up the screen. I took that photo of her when we were in the London Eye. She'd worn blue feather earrings, brown eyes lit by morning sun, a squint that dimpled her cheek. I remember thinking that if I could have ever fallen in love with her it would have been in that moment.

But I didn't.

I silenced my phone, pulled out a Xanax prescription bottle that rattled with pills that would make me sleep. My fingers trembled as a beige pill landed in my palm. I tossed it back and picked up my phone, tapping the Instagram app. I searched Ori's name—as I had done many times before—found her profile and scanned through her memories. It occurred to me then that someone could have found her through Instagram and stalked her. Her account wasn't private, which allowed me to see so many pictures of her, smiling, eating ice cream with her friends, collecting beer can tops left at the river by weekend partygoers.

I remember doing that too. Combing through campsites for strangers' souvenirs. I found a twenty-dollar bill once...bought a band T-shirt with it, which Michael stole and Laurel wouldn't make him give it back.

More pics of Ori standing at the ocean with her friends— one of her friends sporting a beautiful hot pink hat setting off her blonde hair—another of Ori sitting in a golf cart with the same girl, a picture of Ori smoking a joint...with Kimber.

"What the hell?" I sat up, rubbing my tired eyes. It might have been a little different if they were just sitting next to each other, but he was hot boxing it to her, their lips touching. She was seventeen at the time, and he was thirty. "Fucking creep."

She had hundreds of photos. Her at the river, especially

Wilford's Cliff, a place in the river that's too dangerous to swim. It has a shit ton of urban legend tales of people drowning or being eaten by something in the water. But despite the tales, young adults crowd the spot each summer, convinced of their immortality.

But the hotbox picture was the only one of Kimber, or any boy for that matter. She didn't even have any photos of herself with Gabe, which was strange but might explain their failing relationship. It was also possible she could have deleted them after their fight, which could have been a good sign for him. That she had time to go through her social and delete their history. If he had chased her down, hurt her, she wouldn't have had time to delete them. Maybe he was telling the truth.

Just before my eyes got too heavy to keep open, I scrolled to a picture that shook me awake. I shot up, brought the phone as close to my face as possible before the image went blurry. I analyzed it, burned the image into my mind so that even if an asteroid crashed straight down on me, I'd never forget it.

A skinned rabbit lying in a pile of brown leaves long fallen. Three taper candles placed into the ground near its head.

"What the fuck, Ori?" I recognized the old dead tree in the background. Passed it a million times on Route 9 when I lived in Sweetwater. The Hager's auto shop was just down the street from the old cypress. If the rabbit was still there, I'd find it. But a feeling rose up, my skin crawling, mind racing. What if Ori hadn't been the person to kill that animal? What if there were others with her at the time? Could they be involved in her disappearance? If so, who were they?

I wanted to tell Shannon about the picture I found on Ori's social. I texted him.

> Hey Shannon, I need to talk to you about Ori's disappearance.

He replied rather quickly:

> I'm listening.

> Are you working tomorrow?

> Yep. I go in at 8 and leave for patrol at 9.

I left him on read.

My phone read 7:27 when I left the motel the next morning. I wanted to scope out the dead cypress tree scene from Ori's social before meeting with Shannon at the police station. When I drove through Main Street, semi-trucks blocked off one side of the road. Some were loaded with carnival rides; some had already been unloaded. I passed slowly, scanning the neon colors painted on rides and game stand boards. A purple hippo kiddy ride bulged from its safety straps. Memories of the town carnival hit...the smell of corndogs and popcorn, cotton candy... all the scents of fairgrounds. Laurel had taken me and Michael one night when we were kids. It was after the first time Barrett had assaulted me. I was convinced she knew what happened, and this was her attempt at an apology.

At the end of Main Street, a banner stretched above, anchored from light poles on opposite ends of the road, announcing the fair's opening day...tomorrow.

Out on a back road, Sweetwater lost in the rearview more than ten minutes ago, I approached the rotted cypress tree—its dead branches like fingers reaching upward a good five feet taller than the surrounding trees—that clued me in to where Ori took the picture of the rabbit. I pulled over, listened for cars coming either way. I was home, the place I'd grown up, and yet I felt as safe as a mouse too close to the dangling cheese. A killer was loose and could be someone Ori knew. They could have been the one to mutilate the rabbit. Maybe she was hanging around a bad group, but if I hurried, I could snap a few pics and be back in my SUV before anyone noticed me.

In the wood line, dark wove a lattice wall around me, folding away the daylight. Kicking through weeds and fallen limbs, I scanned for the ritual site but reached the cypress tree without finding it. It had to be near. First though, I wanted a few pictures of the tree I'd thought so much about the last ten years. It was twisted and blackened by the scorch of lightning and even with all the odds against it, remained. Albeit different, the core of the tree still existed.

Like me...I had been struck by a different kind of lightning, and I was still alive. The tree and I were connected in a way no one could understand...unless they'd been through hell too. I knelt by the tree, the cursed cypress that drew in folks who believed they could conjure dark magic from it. I was disappointed Ori had fallen in with those idiots.

I dusted the ground for biting things and then lay down, my camera lens pointed upward, following the trunk that knotted and twisted toward the dancing canopy. Click click click, a series of snapshots filing into the SD card, safe and secure, forever there. The tree would not be forgotten even after it withered itself into a goo of swamp mulch.

There was too much ground debris to find the site with a quick scan. I'd have to stomp down thigh-high weeds and wildflowers in search, not to mention strands of an old barbwire fence, parts of it still nailed to posts. I began pushing soft green stalks down with my shoes, stepping forward in a pattern that lay straight, outward from the tree trunk. I'd walked back to the tree and then out again a few times before a dark spot caught my eyes. A few feet away lay the animal, a rabbit. In Ori's photo, it'd been pinned to the dirt with sticks and vines, rudimentary yet sophisticated.

Now though, it was lying over a tree stump marked with what looked like a word written in blood. I knelt, brushed away some leaves to read it.

"Michael," I whispered. What the actual fuck, Ori?

I lifted my camera and snapped a few pictures from different angles. I stepped closer, the possibility of a discovery that could lead me to Ori stoking these flames of courage. My heart wanted to close up shop, go hide somewhere safe. Because I wasn't safe out here, alone. Dahlia was murdered and my sister was missing...was any girl safe anywhere in Sweetwater?

A car honked, whizzed by in a rusty streak, and my shoulders shot up to my ears, my heart pitching in my throat, and I bolted for the SUV, rising panic blurring the world. My heart raced and fear took over and I ran faster, without taking the care I should have. My foot caught a string of barbwire fencing and I tripped, face smacking the wet, dank ground.

I lifted my head, a skid mark of dirt from eye to chin stinging my face, a nice scratch from the barbs running down my arm. "Ugh." I spat, knelt up, frantically wiped the swamp stink off my face. I held up the cut, blobs of blood pooling where the spikes dug in deeper. I couldn't remember when I'd had my last tetanus shot. "Shit."

I'd ran back to my car, pulled the door shut, my finger pressed the lock button so hard it hurt, but I was safe from the scary world. "Fuck." I exhaled, sharp and forceful, trying to expel the fear spray-foamed inside my chest. My fingers trembled to grab my phone from my purse. I flipped it right-side up and started dialing the number for the police department, but a glance back at the woods, the tree line seeming to creep nearer and nearer, pushed me to drive off, tossing the phone in the passenger's seat so I could flip a U-turn and head back to town.

The image of the site scrolled through my mind constantly until I put the car in park in the drug store parking lot, wiping off the dirt on my face with a balled-up napkin from the glove box.

I pulled open the door, careful not to announce my entrance, but in small towns it was almost impossible to blend in, especially when your name was Johnna LaGrange. The aisle with antiseptic products was all the way in the back, and by the time I'd wormed my way through the store to find it, a few customers had spotted me, mumbling to each other under their breath. I kept my head down, pushed past them, wished I hadn't heard syllables sounding like "sister" and "murder." I snatched a basic medical kit and walked to the register where I was greeted by a middle-aged woman, hair fraying out of a bun that looked thrown together without much care.

She scanned my item, the restraint to keep from asking me questions visibly snuffed on her face. I hadn't made it to the door before the patrons ascended on the cashier in hopes for the "tea." Not today, nosey Nancies.

In my car, I wiped clean my face and was happy to see no visible marks underneath the dirt smudge on my cheek. But my arm was a different story. I tried to remember the last time I had a tetanus vaccine but came up with nothing. If I cared at all about my health I'd have gone to the Med Express, but the urgency to seek treatment was pushed out of my mind by the gnarly shit I'd just seen in the woods.

I was not willing to believe Ori had anything to do with it, but I didn't know her the way I should. As her big sister and sworn protector, I failed her. First, I find she's hanging out with a bad crowd and now she's cutting up animals and using them for wicked shit she had no business meddling in.

Satisfied with the wrap I'd placed over the fencing gash, I headed over to the local print shop. I wanted physical copies and didn't want to drive all the way to Belhaven to get them done at Walmart.

The door there dinged too when I walked in. Satellite radio played low through a mounted corner speaker, something indie rock and unfamiliar.

"I'll be right with you," a voice said from a back room. A young girl, arms filled with boxes, high-school, maybe first year of college, big brown eyes lightly dusted with silver glitter, cherry sheen lips. There was a warm, familiar feeling about her.

The boxes slapped the floor with a thud when she dropped them next to a machine. And then she made eye contact, paused, her smile straightening. "You're Ori's big sis, Johnna, right?"

I cleared my throat, surprised to hear mention of my sister's name. "Yeah, I am." And then it clicked, why I knew the girl. "You're Lexi. I knew you looked familiar."

"I go by Alexis now. I didn't think you'd remember me, though." She flicked the box cutter in her hand, skimmed it along the edges of a package. "I heard it's official."

I wasn't sure what she meant and shot her quizzical look.

"That Ori's a missing person."

For the first time ever, I was glad word traveled fast in small towns. The more people who knew, the more eyes there would be on the lookout for my sister.

"Any news yet?" Her sweet face looked at me, expectant, hopeful.

"We haven't heard anything yet. I was going to ask if you had any until you gave me that look." I didn't want to give her hope by saying *I know she'll turn up* when I really didn't know if she would. "You guys still BFFs or did y'all grow apart in the last ten years?"

Her expression deepened, sadness pulling down the corners of her mouth. "We were...until she started hanging around Dahlia."

"Dahlia Cochran?" I confirmed.

She nodded.

"Was Dahlia not someone you approved of?"

She nodded again.

Alexis's judgment held weight; I trusted her opinion because I had grown up trusting her family and if she knew Dahlia well enough to not trust her, then she might know where Dahlia lived. "You got an address for me?"

"Just off Cattail Road," she offered in a snap.

My heart sank. A lot of criminal shit happened in that neck of the woods. *Why the hell was Ori down there?* "In the trailer park?"

"Yeah. Dahlia was living there with an old lady."

"What old lady?"

"I don't know. Her aunt I think, but it's the only trailer with flowers planted around it."

I pulled out my camera. "I want to get these pictures I just took printed, but..." I wasn't sure I should tell her what I'd photographed in the woods, but she'd see the photos anyway. "They are disturbing, so if blood or bone or freaky shit in general triggers you, then I'll get them done somewhere else. I don't want to—"

"It's fine. Thanks for asking." Her expression was peak interest. "What exactly will I be looking at when they are finished?"

I blew out a breath for a little too long, not wanting to bring her into whatever shit I might have been stumbling into. "It looks like a ritual setting. A rabbit, skinned, lying on a stump. Lots of blood and sinew." I wasn't going to have her print the ones with Michael's name on them, so she didn't need to know about that.

She stilled. "Oh."

"Anything else like it been found around here?"

Her lips still held the O-shape, eyes locked on the SD card I'd proffered. "Yeah. I mean no," she stammered. "I mean I haven't seen it for real, but I've heard people talk about seeing it." She held the card loosely. "I um—"

I leaned against the counter, folded my arms together. "Who have you heard talking about it?"

The printer's internal components clicked as the system switched on. "People, ya know." Her eyes dropped down, pretended to look at the printer's display screen.

"People like Ori?"

She sighed, casting an exhausted look at me. "Ori didn't do stuff like that. Not that I ever knew. She mostly just practiced earth magic things, like manifestation and such."

A smile stalled at the corners of my mouth. "She finally putting that intuition to good use, huh? How long?"

"Since middle school. We practiced together sometimes."

I nodded. "That's sweet. Your momma used to tell me ghost stories about the woods near the farmhouse. Scared the piss out of me, but I always begged her to tell me more."

"Me too. I still don't like the woods coz of her," she said, snatching up the test-run copy and tossing it in the trash.

"Well, she told a good story that's for sure." The room went quiet for a second. "Does your momma still work with hospice?"

She shook her head, loading a stack of photo stock into the machine. "She's working at the county hospital now. Has been for about eight years." Printed pictures filed out and the machine hummed to a stop. She lifted them into a paper holder and handed them to me. "Here, you check them. If they have anything to do with Ori, I don't want that image to pop in my head every time I think about her."

"I understand." I took them, tucked them in my purse. "How much do I owe you?"

"Don't worry about it. This is my dad's store. He'd want me to give them to you."

I smiled as best I could; the ability was slipping farther away each minute Ori was still missing. "Give your momma a hug for me? And thank your dad." I opened the door.

"I sure will. Stop in and see me again?"

"Sure." I didn't know if I would or not, but for now, *sure* was the word of God.

I stepped out into the heat, breath catching in my throat. North Carolina summers could choke an elephant. I tapped the outside of my purse, feeling the bulge of the pictures as if they might've disappeared in the fifteen feet I'd walked from the shop to my SUV. *Still there.* I wasn't sure yet if I wanted to take this to the police not knowing what might come out about Ori. Or they might think I was looking for clues that weren't there, wasting their time with nonsense.

But Michael's name on that stump and Kimber's threat about things getting worse for my brother kept drilling the back of my brain, a woodpecker's beak on the trunk. I made up my mind that I'd show the pictures to Shannon. I put my SUV in drive and headed for the station.

CHAPTER NINE

The smell of coffee and Pine-Sol smacked me in the face when I pushed through the double doors and into the police station lobby. An older guy with short gray hair and beard manned the reception desk. He looked up at me with a reassuring smile that said, *Yes, you are safe here*—even though the only other place worse than there was the farmhouse.

I shook my leg, stopped when I heard the water cooler glugging, saw the reception guy side-eyeing me. I hated police stations, been to my fair share, mostly as a teen, once as an adult. Well, once before this trip home, but who was counting?

The shuffling of feet, an audible laugh. Shannon emerged from the back hall. "Hey," he said, a bit too chirpy for this early in the morning.

I smiled. "Hey, Shannon"—I looked at the reception guy—"Can we go somewhere and talk?"

"Sure." He led me to a nearby room, opened the door, and gestured at me to enter before him. "So—" he closed the door—"How's Sweetwater treating its returning celebrity?"

I was far from famous, but...small towns. I flexed my writing hand. "I don't know how many more autographs I can sign."

He teased a laugh, which was some form of relief. His mood seemed much lighter now than it had before. "You'll inform me if anyone harasses you?"

Ah, there was the serious Shannon from yesterday. I shook my head. "I'm serious, Johnna. Folks get riled up when girls are getting killed."

My head split. "You mean *girl*," I corrected, nearly uppercutting him with a verbal assault. "Right? Have you heard some—"

"No, it's just Dahlia." He shook his head like a cat out of water. "Sorry. That was careless of me."

The ringing in my ears instantly subsided. Anyway, I didn't believe these folks cared about any of this. If they were so riled up, why weren't they helping me look for Ori? I wanted to show him the picture of Kimber and Ori, and the one of the dead animal, but decided to start with my theory on Gabe. I opened my phone and went to Ori's social media. "See, there's no photos of her and Gabe," I said, after scrolling through her pictures. "How would she have time to delete them if he chased her down after their argument?"

"Well," he cocked his head. "If he had her phone, he could have done it."

Shit. "I didn't think about that." Then it occurred to me. "He called me!" I grabbed Shannon's arm.

He looked down at the fingernails digging into his arm. "And?"

I yanked away my grip. "He never had my number. The only way he could have gotten it was from Ori's phone. He must have it. We have to go over there and ask him."

Shannon shook his head. "There's no *we*. The police will handle it."

I dropped my phone to my waist. "So, what are you going to do about it?"

He squeezed the bill of his hat, snuggled it down on his head. He was wearing the hell out of that uniform and a tingle shot between my legs and fluttered in my stomach. "I'm going to see how Gabe got your number." He threw up his hands. "If she's even missing."

I wanted to punch him in the face; the urge to ravish him dead just then. "What do you mean *if*? You know something's wrong, right? Doesn't that cop instinct tell you something is wrong?"

He lowered his head, chewed his bottom lip. "Yeah." His eyes slowly rose to meet mine. "I'm catching something is off, but Ori's left before...took off to the beach, off to New York City for a few days. So, this doesn't seem so out of left field to me. Sorry."

He really didn't believe me. That hurt a little. I needed to show him the pictures. "I found something in the woods out on Route 9. Thought you might want to look at it."

"Alright." He eyed me as I sifted through my bag, methodically opened the envelope, and pulled out the small stack of photos. His stare never felt so awful as it had then. The narcissist in me truly thought I'd win him over as soon as he saw me. That he would forgive me for ghosting him all those years ago. It was clear he hadn't.

"There's something in there you're going to want to see." I watched his expression as he flipped through them, trying to read if I'd made a bad decision in showing them to him. I noted the shift in his face when he saw the picture of the skinned rabbit.

He flipped the picture around to show me. "Where did you find this?"

I pointed in the direction. "By the old cypress off Route 9."

He shook his head. "You shouldn't have gone there alone."

Suddenly I was nauseous with panic. "Why?"

He leaned in, seeming to examine the cut on my brow. "You aren't thinking right."

Well, aren't you Captain Obvious? "No shit, Shannon. My sister is missing, and her best friend was murdered, and I'm supposed to carry on like it's all unicorns and rainbows? I'll do whatever I have to do to find her." I stared at him deadpan while my mind mutilated itself with images of my sister, splayed over an old cypress, sludge-covered and swamp isolated, the deep reds of her sinew glinting off pinholes of sunlight.

He gave back the pictures, plunged his hands into his pockets. "I think it's best the police take it from here."

"And what does that look like?" I shoved the pictures into my bag.

"I'll tell the sheriff what you showed me...see what he thinks. We'll get an announcement to the community; anyone sees anything they need to report it. That kind of thing."

"And what about Michael?" There was a reason his name was on that stump. Why else would someone skin a rabbit and paint his name with its blood? "Someone wants to hurt him."

"Johnna"—He put his hands on my shoulders—"No one is after your brother."

I pulled away. "You can't possibly know that."

He stepped closer, an intent in his eyes that drove me wild. He gripped my arms gently, dragged his hands down them until he found my hands and then gave them a reassuring squeeze. "I'm going on patrol; I'll stop by Gabe's house. Meanwhile, I'll have headquarters search for the last ping on Ori's phone. Maybe that'll stir up something useful." He craned his neck down, his face so close to mine. "We'll find her. I promise."

Shannon had finally let down his wall and I let the chemistry pull me closer, our lips nearly touching before I pulled away. "I want to go with you."

His brows furrowed. "To Gabe's?"

"Yes."

He shook his head. "We've been through this already. You can't go."

Jesus fucking Christ. "Fine." I stepped back, hoped my cheeks weren't as red as they felt. "I'll go get some posters made, start hanging them around town and along Route 9."

He nodded and opened the door for me, an affront of coffee and disinfectant on my nose again.

***

At the print shop, a sulky guy with too much hair and not enough deodorant lifelessly greeted me.

"Hi." I approached the register where he stood, phone sideways, thumbs going at some video game. I would have rather spoken to Alexis, but I guess she was covering for this guy when I'd come in earlier. I was disappointed though, since I was hoping to talk to her again about Ori's friends.

"What do ya need?" he asked, setting his phone on the counter.

I thumbed through my phone, found the graphic I'd made already and then flipped the screen to him. "I need some flyers made. The girl in the photos is missing."

"No shit?" His tone was so genuine that I couldn't be angry at his casual response.

"No shit." I pulled my phone away. "Do I just email it or—"

"Nah." He skipped around the counter and rushed up to me, reaching out a hand for my phone. "I can just plug it into the printer and go from there. Get you a bunch of these in no time." He sounded so proud.

"Okay." I gave him my phone, realizing just then how awkward it felt to hand it over to a perfect stranger.

He plugged it in, and the machine whirred to life and paper started popping out. "How many you want?"

"Umm...a hundred." I had no idea if that was enough or too much.

"Alright." We were both silent for a second and then. "So, who is she?"

I swallowed. "My sister." The machine hummed as it started spitting out copies.

He plucked one of the posters up, turned it over. A quality check maybe. "She's really pretty."

"And she knows it." Ori would tell me how pretty I was and then say, *but not as pretty as me* and we both knew she was right.

The printing finished and he packed them in a box for me. "I hope you find her," he said, handing me the receipt.

I'd purchased a staple gun at the local hardware store, staved off a bunch of questions from the nosy old lady who cashed me out, and had one side of Main Street done—with the help of some very kind volunteers—before a loud vehicle pulled up next to me. I looked over, irritated at the disturbance, and wanted to fold in on myself. "Kimber." An acknowledgment of his existence was all I could offer him.

"Johnna, my new favorite person." His tone was nothing if not sarcastic. He sat in his truck, letting it idle loudly next to me.

"That so?" I stapled the poster and walked down to the next pole, Kimber driving alongside me.

"So, why does Ori have a picture of you and her basically kissing on her social?"

His truck chugged, almost stuttering for him. "What are you talking about?"

"You know what I'm talking about."

"I really don't." He dragged out the word *really*.

I wanted to spit in his face; instead, I plucked a few posters and leaned in through his passenger window, plopping them in the seat. "You want to help out and hang those?" Fucking asshole hadn't even offered.

He looked down, arched an eyebrow. "Yeah, sure." He did a kind of two-fingered salute and drove away, and I was glad of it. My ribs started spasming and my stomach pitched; hanging up posters of my missing sister wasn't good enough. I needed to know something, to hear something from someone. Shannon should have been back from Gabe's house by now, so maybe he had some information that would rid me of this doom settling in my gut.

I grabbed a bitter cup of joe at the fast-food drive-thru and drove to a spot where I could drink it and text Shannon. The closest place with privacy was the back of the old milk plant, a spot I used to hang out at when I was in middle school. We'd smoke weed and throw rocks at the silos and tell creepy stories. A few years later, Tracey Carrington got a car and we relocated to the river where we chilled in bikinis and sweated over each other's bodies.

Drizzle dusted the windshield...I kept the wipers off because it wasn't enough rain to keep them from squeaking over the glass. I pulled out my phone and texted Shannon.

> Hey. I was hoping you could fill me in on your visit with Gabe.

Immediately, texting dots appeared. And then vanished. I waited ten minutes, took a few hits from my Sneak-a-Toke, and went to Ori's social media again, scrolling to the pictures of her at the river. She smiled in all her selfies, in every picture that bright, wide smile was a false beacon because her eyes told a different story. I recognized that masking technique, used it every day all my life, big smile to hide the pain. But what was she so unhappy about, other than the obvious...living with an alcoholic mother and sibling. Barrett had never touched her. I made sure of that. I would take it all over again just to make sure she didn't.

I was about to drive off when I saw Kimber's truck speed by, Michael in the passenger seat, bottle in hand. "It's not even noon and you're already drinking." I grit my teeth, put my paraphernalia back in the console and pulled out to follow them, but before I got out of the parking lot my phone buzzed. It was Shannon.

Sorry. I got an emergency response call.

I don't recall hearing sirens.

Is everything okay?

Yeah. Same shit different day.

So, was the visit with Gabe productive?

If it had been, he'd have probably led with that.

Nope.

Goddamnit.

Why not?

That was bitchy, but fuck it. I wanted to know.

> Sticking to his story that she left after they argued, and he didn't go after her. Says he doesn't have her phone either. Still waiting on her phone records.

> How'd he get my number, Shannon?

> He said he got it from Ori's phone a while back.

So, he's a creep. I remembered the pictures on Ori's social of her at the river.

> Want to go to the river with me when you get off work? Maybe we can find something there?

It was a long shot but still.
More dots, then nothing, then dots, then nothing. Then...

> Sure. I'll pick you up at the motel when I get off work.

I couldn't remember if I had told him I was staying at the motel, but I didn't want to go down a rabbit hole of paranoia. Not with him. He was Shannon, the person who'd always had my back. He knew everything about me when I lived at home.

> No, I'll pick you up. Text me your address.

> You already know it 🙂

I was confused for a second then it hit me.

> You still live at Crooked Run?

> Yep.

> Okay. Text me when you're ready.

I waited for a reply of a thumbs up and then another text popped up.

It was from Laurel.

> I'm not feeling well. Can you pick up my prescription from the drug store and bring it to me?

Just what I wanted to do.

> I'm busy. Michael can't run out for you?

> He's at work. That's all that boy does. You know that. Can you get it for me or not?

I really didn't fucking want to.

> Yeah Momma. I'll be there soon.

She was probably severely hungover, but just in case she had a cold, I figured I'd grab some Ny-Quill.

My tires slid around every turn that snaked through the woods for half a mile before opening to the farmhouse. The contents of the drugstore bag jostled and fell off the seat onto the floorboard, the green liquid medicine sloshing inside the plastic bottle.

I remembered Ori being sick when she was little. I brought her up a dose in a plastic shot glass. Laurel was leaving to party for the night, so it'd be just me there taking care of her. I helped Ori sit up, gave her the medicine, and changed out a rag on her head that had gone hot.

I sat with her all night until I heard Laurel stumble through the door, heels clacking on the hardwoods, laugh echoing in the foyer, and, when she didn't come upstairs to check on Ori, I stayed longer...until the sun came up and Ori woke with her fever broken. She smiled and hugged me, said thanks for watching over her all night. I told her I'd always watch out for her, and now she was gone. I made a liar out of myself really good. But she made it easy for me.

I swallowed a lump of guilt and walked inside the house. "Momma?" Laurel didn't answer. I crept into the kitchen, the living room...she wasn't there. She must be out of it to still be in her room. I ran up the stairs, not giving a thought to the memories they triggered, and stopped at Laurel's door, taking a deep breath before knocking.

"Johnna? That you?"

"Yeah, Momma."

"Well come in then." Her tone was a snake bite.

I turned the knob, opened the door slowly, trying hard not to think about the times I was made to walk into that room, the nights Laurel was out with her girlfriends, tearing up the town and not giving two shits that her daughter was being assaulted.

"Ahem," I cleared my throat of the bile creeping up. Her room smelled of garlic and sweat, the way a person smells after heavy drinking all night. "I've got your medicine." I reached in the white paper bag that read Sweetwater Pharmacy in blue.

Laurel coughed, her head beaded in sweat, perspiration a dark spot on the pillow. "How much was it?"

I pulled out two bottles, Xanax and Ativan. Nothing that would bring down her fever. "$52.83"

She pulled her knees into the fetal position. "You can deduct it from all I spent raising ya." Her face was clammy, like waterlogged skin after swimming too long. She needed to be washed, or at least wiped down.

"Okay, Momma." I walked to her bathroom, searched

through the cabinets and found a washcloth. I wetted it in cold water and held it on her head, just like I had for Ori.

"What were you doing all day today?" Laurel asked, her hands slapping the bedside table for the empty cigarette pack.

The last thing she needed was to light up, so I pushed it out of her reach. "I had posters made for Ori...hung them around town."

She grabbed my arm, squeezed it hard. "Why the hell'd you do that?" she spat.

There was no use in explaining; she was barely coherent. Her grip loosened quickly, a weak hand flopping down to the sheets.

I left Laurel once she passed out. The cold meds took longer to kick in, but eventually I crept out.

CHAPTER TEN

I still had time before I was meeting Shannon, so I decided to take a trip to the trailer park where Dahlia lived. *Used to live.*

The dirt road was pocked with rain-filled potholes; I'd need to hit up a car wash afterward to keep anyone from asking about the flung mud all over my car. The road was lined with bowed pines and flood waters that lapped at edges of the road.

Mist rolled in between the trees as the heat intensified and began to evaporate the swamp. I rolled my window down to listen to the frogs. They were always croaking in the swamps, day and night. The smell of rot and renewal mixed in the air, and I breathed it in, remembering a childhood of swamp frolic. Most people would think it absurd to let your children play in the swamps, but Laurel didn't care where I went, and the only place that felt safe was the woods.

The road opened to the trailer park. Slender, aluminum, rectangles sat diagonal to the road, small lots of grass separating each one. Giant limbs reached into some of the abandoned homes, windows busted, fallen canopy denting in the roofs. The park seemed an island in the bog; like in another decade the swamp would swallow it whole. I searched each one for the planted flowers Alexis mentioned—most of the yards were barren mud holes. A barrel billowed black smoke from the backyard, reminding me of the tractor tires Barrett would burn. Sun rays glinted through holes in the canopy like so many camera flashes, and between honey orange bursts of light, I saw the trailer.

Rickety, waterlogged steps creaked under my weight, and the porch landing swayed when I stepped on it, like a wobbling table in need of a thrice folded napkin under one leg.

"Hello," I said, as I rapped my knuckles on the door, careful not to touch the mildew growing all over it. Climates like this were notorious for breeding mildew...it's like even the Earth wants to absorb this land, rid itself of the blemish.

The sudden twist of silver doorknob, a crack and a pale, tired face peering out as the dark slit in the door widened. "Can I help you?"

The distant look in her eyes and her feeble voice caught me by surprise. This was not a place for feeble women. It was hardcore or tail between the legs running in this neck of the woods. But there she was in spite.

I gathered my thoughts and proffered a hand to shake. "Hi. I'm Johnna LaGrange. My sister is missing, and I know she and Dahlia were friends. Do you—"

Her eyes brightened like Ed McMann was on her doorstep. "Are you with the police, honey?" The woman's hopeful desperation was a taloned claw grip to my gut.

My thoughts slammed against the front of my skull and bounced back in shambles, questions splayed about like interstate roadkill and all I could say was, "Yes, ma'am." I couldn't stop the lie. It was too easy.

She stepped aside. "Come in."

I looked back to my SUV, its safety meaningless from here. "Are you home alone?"

She frowned. "It's just me."

Oh shit. I'm such a jerk. Of course it's just her...Dahlia is dead.

"Thank you," I said, taking the glass of lemonade rattling in front of my face, old hands unstable. I took a sip, mostly to be nice, but my mouth was already Texas dry and old ladies made good lemonade. The iced, tangy-sweet drink slid down my throat like an arctic wind. I smiled. "That's delicious."

She fluffed a pillow into the back of an old rocking recliner. "So, have you come with news on a suspect?"

This was my first-class ticket to hell, for sure. "No, Miss...?"

"Call me Beverly, honey." She leaned forward and patted my knee.

I winced at her cold touch. "Huh," I gasped, then played it off with easy banter. "You must have the world's warmest heart."

"Oh, ha!" she trilled. "I've got a lot of love in there."

I moved back to the point quickly. "Beverly, can you tell me if you've ever seen this girl?" I held up my phone, a picture of Ori glowing from it.

She examined it carefully. "Yes. I believe that's Dahlia's friend, uh..."

"Ori," I verified.

She nodded. "Yes, that's right. Ori Kern. What a sweetheart, that girl."

Too sweet to be gallivanting the woods with your psycho niece. "When was the last time you saw her?"

Her face twisted in confusion. "Who?"

"Ori." I was close to getting some answers and adrenaline surfed my nerves.

"Hmm, let me think." She pushed stray hairs behind her ears and cupped the fraying bun at the base of her neck checking it was still fashioned securely. "Saturday night I think?"

I nearly choked on my tongue. "The 13th?"

"Yes, hun. It was Ori's graduation, and Dahlia's birthday. The two were getting dolled up here." Beverly looked down the hall; I craned my neck to follow. Ominously dark, the hallway stretched long and stopped at a darkened door. "That Dahlia's room?"

"Sure is," she said, voice trembling.

The fact that my questions were causing this woman pain wasn't lost on me, but I still didn't have answers. "How long did she live with you?"

Beverly closed her eyes and tears spilled. "All her life. Dahlia's mother birthed her in prison and she's still there."

I itched to see inside Dahlia's bedroom, sure I'd find something that would lead me to Ori. It was rude as hell to ask, but, "Mind if I have a look?" I nodded toward the bedroom door.

Beverly stood, quick as a cat jumping from a hot stove and motioned for me to follow. "Sure, honey. If it helps find her killer, I don't think she'd mind people in her room."

Her silhouette shrank as we poked down the dark hall, the wood paneling suffocating any light that traveled in from the front door's diamond shaped window.

Dahlia's room was exactly as I pictured. Poor knew what poor looked like, and a poor girl (if they were lucky) had the bare minimum: something that constituted a bed, a smallish dresser or old storage bin for clothes and a secret hiding place for all the stolen shit that'd get you a whoopin' if they were found. I looked over my shoulder at the sound of the door gently closing, Beverly behind it. She wanted to give me space.

I hated lying to her, but I couldn't forget the police officer's jokes about Dahlia and how she was just a trouble-seeker. The cops weren't looking for her even before they knew she was dead. Would they look for Ori? My face flushed hot with anxiety. I had to find something here, though tearing through a dead girl's private belongings felt wrong. My fingers traced over a picture Dahlia had stuck on the side of her dresser mirror: her and Michael kissing while he took the selfie. My lips tugged into a soft frown, the sweet innocence of young love.

I moved across the room, sat on the edge of her bed while trying to imagine her life. That was the hard part, constructing a scenario of someone I didn't know. But I knew if I tried, I could. If anyone could relate to a shit life, that was me, and from the policewoman's comments it was safe to assume Dahlia knew a thing or two about the shit life could shovel onto a person. My eyes were drawn to the headboard tattooed with graffiti. I leaned closer, catching the names Michael and Dahlia inside a heart, the text a flourish similar to calligraphy, short lines of poetry and quotes, all in that same sweeping font, one in particular I recognized. *I could bear those hypocritical smiles no longer! I felt that I must scream or die!*

Edgar Allan Poe's *A Tell Tale Heart*. "Dramatic," I said, for no other reason than the need to hear someone's voice in the uncomfortably quiet stranger's room...even if it were my own. Poe's work was my escape as a teen. I read everything he'd ever written time and time again, which is why the line scratched into her headboard shook me. Madness birthed from guilt. What was Dahlia feeling guilty about? My stomached flipped as my mind loaded so many reasons Dahlia's murder related to Ori's disappearance. I didn't want to think that the two were connected, but one was dead, and one was missing, and my gut told me it was related, even if I had no proof. Then I noticed a carving. A picture. A symbol I'd seen drawn in rabbit blood at the site by the big tree. The puzzle pieces were growing in number, only I didn't know what the picture was supposed to be.

A red glass perfume oil bottle sat on the nightstand and my curiosity sent my hand to the crucifix-shaped lid, lifting out the oil stem. I drew it to my nose and inhaled the scent of nostalgia, a raining fall evening, wool coats and brick. "Amber oil," I said, gently sliding the stem back into the bottle. Lying next to the bottle was a small black book, and while everything in my body screamed that I was invading her privacy, I couldn't stop my finger from pushing into the bookmarked seam and flipping it open. The words "love spell" were scribbled at the top and a line of text read *the blood of the dead, the name of the living*. I shook my head, rattling the pieces together. The love spell, the skinned rabbit...Michael's name. But the writing on the stump didn't match Dahlia's fancy penmanship. So, who the hell wrote his name on that stump if it wasn't her?

My phone buzzed. I saw it was Shannon and texted back *on my way* before thanking Beverly for her graciousness and leaving for the woods.

I could drive to Shannon's with my eyes closed...this time was different though. Storms had taken down trees that used to be landmarks, and the old tobacco barn, that was once faded red and dilapidated, was now a charred ash pile too forgotten to have been bulldozed over. There was a sadness in its loneliness and something oddly familiar in its mood...like it reflected a part of me that had no name, only emotion. I couldn't pass up the photo op.

I pulled over, the tall roadside grass flattening under my tires. The sun was blotched by dark clouds, a humid breeze rustling in the tree line. It would make for a beautiful picture. I grabbed my camera, carefully crossed a battered barbwire fence loosened from its rotted pole by a decade's neglect, and approached the burnt ruins. The air smelled like wet grass and field weeds fully blossomed, whites and yellows in a waist-high sea of sour bloom.

The sound of my camera clicking was amplified among the wilds...a clear, if not deliberate, reminder that I was out of place. I swallowed the acid in my throat, my body's way of constantly alerting me to its state of imbalance. Like I needed a reminder.

The smell of burnt wood wafted with the wind, and I wondered how long the smell would linger...how long it had lingered. Would it remain, a ghost of a place that once had purpose? My dad used to work tobacco fields, which was why I made it my job at the age of thirteen. Pulling weeds in a tobacco field wasn't exactly fun, but it was time away from home, from Barrett; and it was money.

I was just about to capture the ruins from another angle when a whisper came, something that sounded more like metal grinding against bone and less like a human...but it was a whisper still the same.

"Help me," it said, in a rasp of clicks that grated my flesh.

I pulled my camera away from my eye and scanned the field, daylight smaller upon the world. Goosebumps pricked my skin and still, I wanted to discount the whole thing...hearing voices in the woods. Everyone who grew up in Sweetwater knew not to talk back to voices in the woods. But how could I ignore the familiarity, however monstrous it sounded?

Help me.

The whisper played over and over again like some haunted recording. But who was I supposed to help? My heart palpitated and my chest ached. How could I ignore what I heard? I didn't have time for any of this. I needed to get Shannon and go canvass the Cape Fear River, which had been Ori's stomping grounds ever since she could get there on her own.

Disturbed, salty that I'd even wasted valuable time by stopping in the first place, I tramped back to my car, tossed my camera in the backseat and sped off.

I drove too fast through the winding woods, potholes shooting me off the trail a few times but I was lucky enough to correct my steering before hitting any of the trees that would have left it totaled and me in worse shape. Shannon's car was in the driveway; he was home and hopefully ready to go. I pulled in next to his police truck and honked.

The front porch light flipped on, and he bolted out the door a second later, hustling down the twelve porch stairs. I was proud to say I'd never fallen down them, not once in the million times I'd used them while I was inebriated. But that was the thing with me and stairs: I was always particularly careful on them.

As Shannon approached, I noticed his expression: heavy if not completely foreboding. Had he heard something about Ori? I jumped out. "What's wrong?"

He stumbled to a stop, a quizzical look, his tongue wetting his lips. His disposition lightened and I recognized all too well the effort in that task. "Nothing," he said, but there was a hint of a question in his tone, like he broke his dad's favorite coffee mug and didn't want to admit it. "Why?"

"You looked like..." What was I going to say? *The look on your face was so awful that I thought you heard something about my sister.*

He sighed, dropped his hand that held a ball cap to his side.

"Your sister is missing, and I got jack shit. It's fucking stressful... she's like a sister to me too, you know?"

Fuck. Am I the asshole here? "Yeah of course I do. I'm sorry. I know you're doing your best, Shannon." I got back into my car, managed a sincere smile through the windshield at him and he walked forward, got in.

"The chief's being a dick about assigning the case because of Ori's past, but Johnna, I swear... I'm doing everything I can to convince him she's missing."

I turned around in the driveway and headed back out to the dirt road that would lead to our search spot. "So what do we do now?"

"We need to get into her phone records, but that's impossible without a warrant, and we can't put out an APB on her or her vehicle until she's considered missing. I'm really starting to think that maybe she did run—"

"No, Shannon. No." My knuckles turned white around the steering wheel. "She didn't run away."

"How do you know that?" He sat up straight in his seat, stared at me, curious. "Why are you so sure she didn't run to get away from all the same shit you ran from?"

I swallowed the angry words ready to burst through the bull gate in my throat, gritted my teeth so hard a piece chipped off. "She didn't go through what I went through, Shannon. I took all of it so she didn't. When Barrett came into the room for her, I didn't pretend to be sleeping. I made him choose me every single time. And if you recall, I didn't leave until after he died. So what could have been so bad here to make her run away?"

His expression changed to one that I'd seen before when we used to talk about the things Barrett had done to me. But then his brows lifted, and he said, "What if she's pregnant?"

I stalled, my mind processing his theory. If she were pregnant, she would have told Gabe, right? "She would have come to me if that were true." There was no reason for me to say that, but I had to convince him she hadn't run away. How was I supposed to feel confident that he could convince his chief to label Ori a missing person if I couldn't convince Shannon without lying? My stomach churned, guilt of being a shitty big sister lodging through me like clogging sewage.

"Are you sure about that?"

Not even a little. Why did he think he knew her better than me? I wanted to yell, but I needed him with me looking for clues at the river, and I didn't want us to end on bad terms after all of this...whatever this turned out to be.

"What about the pictures of the dead animal with Michael's name? He could know something, Johnna. We need to talk to him."

I shook my head. "Just because his name was at that site doesn't mean he knows anything. Girls can be weird when they get jealous. I don't want to stir up a bunch of shit for him. He's already got enough heat because he was Dahlia's boyfriend. If it gets out, this town will crucify him."

"I have to talk to him." Shannon wasn't convinced. His eyes went blank, and he stared at me like I had three heads. "Johnna, look...we're going to have to reveal those pictures to the investigating team anyway. Isn't it better that we talk to your brother first?"

I didn't even know what I was hoping for Michael to say because, honestly, finding something and finding nothing were equally bad.

Shannon exhaled, refusing defeat. "I know this is awful, Johnna. I'm sorry for all of it."

I didn't want his apology; I wanted Ori back. "Fine. But let me talk to him. He won't say shit to you or anyone at the station."

At the riverbank, I pulled the parking brake and watched my footing getting out, my Vans sinking in mud. I blinked to adjust my vision in the fading light.

"I forgot how quickly it gets dark at the river. We'd better hustle," I said, aware that the window for our search was smaller than I'd wanted.

The trail to the riverbank was overgrown; shit grew fast out here and that made me worry. How quickly could evidence be ruined by weeds and mud? Would we find anything at all—even if there were anything to find?

We both acted like we'd never been to the river's edge before, our knees wobbling and limbs flailing to keep steady footing. What a decade could do to muscle memory was surprising. So, what was his excuse? "I thought you'd be able to traverse this place with the grace of a water snake. You're out of practice." I let out a light chuckle then added, "That job keeping you too busy for some good ole river adventures?"

He huffed a laugh. "Nope. But my job has shown me what happens to people out here. More than you'd ever think. It kind of opens your eyes. You'd know better than anyone."

"Yeah, but my dad's drowning was a normal case of someone who got too drunk and lost a game of sink or swim."

We grew up hearing all the tea of people drowning or nearly drowning from falling in or having their tubes or kayaks turn upside down. "How many can there be that the news doesn't spread all over the place?"

"A lot has changed since you and I called this place our stomping grounds. Tourists found our little town right after you left, and the shit that goes down with out-of-towners is mind-blowing."

I hadn't thought about that. But with all the new strangers…

"Do you think a tourist could have had something to do with Ori's disappearance?"

He carefully stepped over a fallen tree limb. "It's more of a possibility than you think."

I stepped to the side and reached down for the other end of the limb, reading his body language of wanting to clear the path to make it safe for others to pass. We lugged it off the path and continued until we were at the landing, a little flat piece of riverbank where it was easy to hang out...set up a tent, which Ori had done several times according to her social media. Daylight was good enough at the river for us to survey the ground without our phone lights. There were rocks and empty beer cans, cigarette butts and cellophane wrappers, but nothing that stood out as evidence of foul play, if Ori had even been here when she went missing. I don't know what I thought I'd find, but nothing was not it.

"Well, no news is good news." Shannon lifted his Tar Heels basketball cap and scratched his sweat-damp hair.

"I guess." I kicked over a crushed pack of menthols with the toe of my shoe, watched a little black water bug scurry over the green and white label. Above us, nesting birds cawed at our intrusion.

I looked down the river's edge, remembered a picture Ori posted on her social media that showed her bending over the ledge of a small cliff, hanging from large piece of driftwood, and in the dimming light I saw it.

I'd been there once, the night my friend's brother, Jonny Wilford, jumped from the ledge; he never made it back up, but he was honored by having the cliff named after him.

"Where are you going?" Shannon asked, his voice cracking in the humid heat.

"To Wilford's Cliff."

"What? No." He hurried next to me.

"Uh...why?" I hardly looked at him and kept walking.

"It's getting dark, Johnna. Let's come back when the sun is out, and we can actually see where we're walking."

"I can see just fine." Until I couldn't and tripped over a tree root. I planted face-first into the mud and slid down toward the rushing river.

CHAPTER ELEVEN

"Shit!" Shannon lunged after me and caught my ankle. "I've got you."

My mouth was crammed with mud, and all I could think about was how that's what it must taste like underneath the water, the taste of grime and dead things. Shannon yanked me up, and before I knew it, I was standing, facing him.

"Are you okay?" He wiped mud off my face with his T-shirt, while I was trying desperately not to look at his sculpted physique, like a character for one of those military shooter games. Damn...he was good looking, more so than I remembered.

My cheeks flushed with heat. "I'm fine." I pushed his shirt back at him and walked toward my SUV, hating very much that me falling proved him right and cut short our scouting mission.

Once we stopped in his driveway, he hopped out and ran around to my door. "Come on," he said, and opened it. "You can shower here, wash your clothes...you don't want to drive all the way back to Laurel's caked in mud and smelling like—"

"I know what I smell like." I put up a hand gesturing for him to stop talking, and he huffed a laugh. "But I'll take the offer.

Laurel might get salty if I come inside the house smelling like river scum."

Inside his house, a lamp he'd turned on before we left barely lit the living room. It sat on a small desk in the back and a picture of his dad's riverboat hung above it. "He sure was proud of that boat," I said, slowly dragging my eyes over the other framed pictures that hadn't moved an inch in over two decades. "So...he just left you this house?"

He paused, then hung his hat on a coat rack. "Yup," he said, and locked the front door. "Come on," he nodded toward the back of the house. "Let's get these muddy clothes in the wash."

I pulled off my muddy shirt, a camisole underneath, and tossed it in the machine. My shorts were muddy too, and I wasn't going to risk stains setting in, so I yanked those off as well.

He laughed. "You never were skittish around me."

I wadded my shorts up and shot them into the washer like a basketball. "You've never given me a reason to be."

His face twitched, and then he closed the lid and pressed the start button. "You want a cold beer?"

"Sure," I said, thinking how great it would be to have a pill to swallow with it. I scanned the living room once more, Ori's disappearance keeping me hyper-focused, eyes wide. Even though I was in a familiar home, the vibe felt different, like a cold hand waiting to grab me from behind. But I couldn't risk missing a clue. No matter where I was, I needed to be looking. I meandered into the kitchen in time to receive an ice-cold bottle of Rolling Rock. "Thanks."

"I got some cold pizza in the fridge if ya want some."

I pulled out a joint, smiled. "I'm going to want it in about ten minutes." I walked over to his trash can and stepped on the pedal to lift the lid. "Hope you don't mind," I said, retrieving an empty beer bottle from the bin so I could use it for an ashtray. I placed the bottle and joint on his kitchen table and brushed my hands over my arms. "It's cold in here."

He pulled out a chair and sat at the table. "Yeah. I'm sorry about that. The AC unit is tricky. It likes one setting, otherwise it gets wonky."

I lit the joint.

He side-eyed me, a coy smile tugging the corner of his mouth. "You know I'm a cop, right?"

"I know you don't give two shits that I'm smoking pot in your house." I took a long drag, tilted my chin to the ceiling and blew out. Another and then I passed it to him.

He shook his head. "I get tested too often for that."

I shrugged. "More for me." I held the joint up to toast his bottle; he obliged, which I thought was dramatically adorable. I took another long drag and then snuffed the end on the beer bottle's lip. "That shower sounds good about now." I stood, scanned the two hallways leading out. I knew there were restrooms either way but wasn't sure which one he preferred I use.

"Follow me. I'll get you a towel and a fresh bar of soap."

The hallway used to have lime green carpet, but now it was solid wood, and as I looked around, I noticed some upgrades he'd made to the place. All the old paneling was gone and the walls were painted in dark blues and grays. A little brooding but soothing.

"Here you are," he said, opening a door and stepping out. "And here is your towel and soap." He walked back into the bathroom and placed them on the sink. I caught him staring at my ass as I leaned over to turn on the shower so it could run the water hot.

"That's a state-of-the-art rain shower system in there." He pointed to the giant square nozzle attached to the ceiling spraying a colossal amount of water

"Cool."

"I'll be in the kitchen." He backed out and shut the door, and I hated the part of me that had wanted him to stay, to undress with me and get in the shower together.

———

He wasn't in the kitchen like he said he'd be, but in his defense, I took a rather long shower. Something about feeling like I was under a gentle waterfall paused all the traumatic shit I was going through, or at least gave me the breath I'd needed since the night Danae tried to kill herself.

"Shannon," I called out. And when I didn't hear anything, I got a prick at the back of my neck, like something sinister had happened to him while I was showering. "Where are you?"

I didn't like this. But the house was big and there were decks outside that had stairs leading down to the river's edge. I opened the door off the kitchen that led out back and stepped into a humid night, cicadas thrumming, frogs croaking. Solar lights dotted the tops of the deck posts, which gave me a sort of relief, as if the lights were an indicator of security. I walked along the deck, peering over to see the lower levels, the winding stairs, but I saw nothing but trees and deck. As my heart began finding its familiar cadence of ninety miles an hour, it dawned on me that he was probably passed out on his bed.

I went back inside, walked down the hallway and peeked into a room I figured might be his. The room was bare but for a small couch and some filled bookshelves. The idea of Shannon reading on that couch, in that room on a rainy day, pulled my lips into a smile.

Down the hall, a door was cracked open, and I remembered that being Mr. Hager's room. I gently urged it wider and peeped through. Once my head was inside, I heard the shower. Then it turned off. I backed out but didn't leave, keeping my eyes on the bathroom door through the slit at the hinges. *Peeping Tom.* Ew.

I walked again to the kitchen and peered out of the screen door that showed all the way down to the docks. I'd ran up and down those two flights of stairs countless times when I was little. My hips rested on the side of the deep freezer plastered in 80s music stickers from Mr. Hager's days. The majority were his favorite band, Metallica.

I bent down, sitting on my heels, and pushed open the screen just enough to shoo out a stink bug. Standing, I looked at the freezer again, memories of popsicles in a tube always there for us when we wanted. Curiosity made me want to open the freezer to see if there were any in there now. I talked myself out of it twice before finding my palm around the handle. I went to lift when I heard, "Hey!"

I jumped and spun around, the freezer door slamming shut. Shannon was standing there, pale as a ghost.

My mouth went dry. Did he have bad news about Ori? "What's the matter?"

"Sorry, I just...I got a call from work."

My heart leapt. "Anything—"

He shook his head before I could finish. "Nah, just some scheduling reshuffles. Vacation season, ya know."

I couldn't hide my disappointment.

"Hey..." He came to the door and leaned next to me on the freezer, scooping an arm around my waist. "There hasn't been any evidence of foul play. Right now, everything points to her being alive, so that's why the investigation should be looking at places alive people would be and not in places you'd find a body, like along the riverbank or the swamps. Just because she made good grades doesn't mean she didn't let her emotions steer her decisions, Johnna. She very well could have bolted for a few days just to get her head together."

God, the sincerity in his eyes could have raised the dead. My heart felt lighter in that moment, and maybe that's why I leaned into him, pressed my lips on his. He jerked back, confused and eager at once. "Are you sure we should do this?"

"You don't want to?"

His gaze crippled me, and then he moved in, his mouth on mine again, his fingers through my hair. His lips pushed harder against mine, forceful and wanting. His hands trembled with excitement...fulfillment, we were that moment just after the Mentos sunk in the soda bottle. He tasted like beer and lust, and I wanted him. He picked me up, arm in the small of my back and his other hand gripping my ass, and sat me on the freezer, his tongue looping around mine.

"Fuck, you're so sexy," he moaned around my mouth. His lips moved up my cheek, nibbled my ear and trailed back down my neck. The string on my cami slipped over my shoulder, his teeth tugging it down further...kissing my collarbone.

I pulled back, lifted my cami up around my arms and threw it...somewhere. When his fingers found the hem of my panties, my body tingled. "Are we really doing this?"

He leaned back, a crease of disappointment in his forehead. "You want to stop?"

"Oh hell no." I pulled him back in, took his hand in mine and led him between my legs. He rubbed me gently, the wetness building...and then his fingers were inside.

A moan of pleasure danced between our lips, and I laid back. He took my nipple in his mouth, his tongue circling it. A bite, gentle and teasing, then lips pecking their way down to my navel, on my clit, sucking and licking, fingers gliding in and out, and I closed my eyes.

"Mm," he grunted, and brought himself over on top of me, pushing his dick inside, my reckless tendencies forgoing a condom. He looked me in the eyes, accomplishment and determination glaring back at me, and whispered, "I want to tear you apart."

I raked my fingers down his back, pulled him as close to me as he could get, our bodies rocking, the freezer knocking the wall with each thrust. "Do it then."

───────

Inside my car, Shannon leaned through the rolled down window and kissed my cheek, the burn of his lips on my scratches making it no less sweet. I still felt his lips there as I drove, my fingers lifting to touch the same place, some fucked-up need to rid myself of the pleasure by wiping away the physical memory. My sister was missing and there I was thinking about Shannon's—

I slammed my brakes, tires sliding in the gravel. "Shiiit!" I jerked the wheel and swerved off the path, narrowly missing a stand of pine trees, and ground to a stop. I whipped my head around to look for the car that had come out of nowhere, their headlights a million lumens straight to my eyes.

"What the hell," I gasped, seeing nothing. I stepped out, listened, only the sound of a wood ready for sleep. Hallucinating was becoming my norm, and I didn't fucking like it. First the shadow outside Ori's bedroom, then the apparition in Laurel's bathroom mirror. What the hell was going on?

I got back in my car, a passing thought of the headlights belonging to one of the Hager brothers—this was their stomping ground after all—and drove toward my motel.

At the light in town, my phone rang. "Hey, Michael, what's up?"

Some scattered sounds came over the line and then, "Can you go check on Momma?" His speech wasn't slurred, but he still sounded off. "I have to take care of some things tonight, and she's in pretty bad shape."

I needed to ask him why his name was written in blood next to a skinned rabbit. A good sister would have gotten rid of the name inked in blood, but *no* not me. I just *had* to take a photograph of it. "Sure. I'll stop over." He hung up then. I tossed the phone on the passenger seat. "You're welcome, turd."

The driveway to Laurel's was rough, the storms had taken a toll on it. Laurel would have already been twirling her hair around her finger to get the road dragged if she weren't sick. She was good at making men do what she wanted. Except for Barrett.

I was nearly motion sick by the time I got out of the car. But the house's vibe set me on edge, and I forgot about the nausea. There was never a reason for the silence that swarmed there, the house was a tidal wave cresting but never breaking.

CHAPTER TWELVE

Michael said Laurel was sick, so I didn't call out when I walked inside the farmhouse, assuming she'd be in bed upstairs. I poked my head into the kitchen, a sink half full of dirty dishes—presumably Michael's—empty beer bottles on the table along with an overflowing ashtray and some car magazines.

I crept upstairs to check on Laurel; her door was ajar. Michael must have left it cracked for me. He'd sat with me through enough panic attacks brought on by the sound of it squeaking open. He knew what Barrett was doing to me but wasn't about to make words with him. I blamed him sometimes for not having my back, but he was younger than me, and I couldn't even stand up for myself.

Laurel was asleep, a half-empty bottle of cold medicine knocked on its side next to her body. It was a different brand, so Michael must have brought her some more. I had no intention of waking her; she was out cold. So...I headed back downstairs to the kitchen, the creaking old house talking to me every step of the way.

"You can fuck right off, you rickety piece of shit." It occurred to me as soon as I heard my own voice that I was talking to the house. I'd never done that before. I wondered if it would listen, since I asked so kindly.

I struggled with the cold-water knob, rust creeping up its edges. I remembered the rust as a kid. It meant nothing to me then. It was just an old sink faucet, so unimportant that no one took interest in cleaning it. But now, the rust made me wither.

I was mostly done with washing the dishes when my hands slipped on the last soapy glass. I fumbled to catch it, but it hit the corner of the sink and shattered, cutting a deep horseshoe shape down the meaty side of my pinky finger. I slapped my other hand over the wound, blood seeping between my fingers, dripping onto the white porcelain sink and splattering into so many blood webs.

"Ungh," I winced, and then my vision went to a scene I couldn't remember happening. *An illuminated tree line approaching at light speed.* I dropped to the floor, squeezing my eyes shut harder, but the scene wouldn't let up. *Blurred lines streaking white and orange across the windshield...blood splatter.* I pounded my forehead with fisted hands, still gripping the wound closed. "Stop it. Stop it. Stop it." I hit harder. "Stoooop," I whimpered. The vision still a blinding horror. "Stop!" I screamed.

When I opened my eyes the image was gone. Just me and the table and a sink filled with dirty dishwater and blood.

I pulled myself up, rummaged through the kitchen cabinets until I found a drawer full of miscellaneous shit that included Band-Aids and antibacterial cream. My hands trembled, Band-Aid on top of Band-Aid and the cut still bled through. Tears pooled in my eyes and when they broke, they found every scratch on my cheek and burned like hell. I yanked a dish towel from the oven door handle and wrapped it around my hand. It'd have to do until I got back into town and hit up the drug store for gauze and medical tape. This town was literally tearing me apart. First the barbwire and now this.

I held my wounded hand to my heart, the rapid rise and fall of my chest ushering in a wave of panic. I started rocking back and forth, my spine smacking the wooden slatted wall. *Breathe, Johnna. Just breathe.* That wasn't helping either. I rushed to my purse hanging on the back of a chair, dug out my Ativan and popped it in my mouth, cold water from the kitchen faucet and it was down. The room was spinning, a high-pitched ringing in my ears, and all I could do was try not to pass out.

I stared blankly at the kitchen curtains above the sink. Little ducks with aprons. They were cute once. Now they barely showed, stained by nicotine.

"What happened to your hand?"

My heart flipped, and I spun around. "Michael!" I huffed out a long breath. "You scared the shit out of me." I faced him, leaning against the sink. "I thought you had things to take care of tonight." I was almost happy to see him until I noticed how much he looked like the house did when I pulled up. Burdened. I wanted out of there. "Well, Laurel is dosed up on cold meds, and I washed your dishes. You're welcome. I'm out."

His brows creased, shoulders slumped forward; he was definitely drunk. He glanced over at the sink, my blood still blotching the counter. "I'll clean it," he said, eyes glazed over, vacant.

I didn't like leaving my blood there for him. Not because I felt guilty that he had to clean it, but because there was something deeply personal about cleaning up someone else's blood. Having my drunk younger brother do it felt wrong...like leaving a diary splayed out to be scrutinized.

Back at my motel room, the hum of the air conditioner a solace, I lay flat on the bed...shoes still on like some swamp goblin. The ceiling fan wobbled, knocking the light pull-chain against the bulb and making the softest clinking noise. I homed in on its rhythm, the way it made a kind of tune...soon words came and before I knew it was singing a mantra I'd just made up, another of my coping mechanisms. I lay there—many moments too long —soothing myself.

Then I sat up, grabbed my phone from my purse and felt guilt and relief when there were no notifications. Danae would be in the observation ward another four days, but she was allowed to make phone calls.

My skin still crawled with the eerie vision that hijacked my brain at Laurel's, headlights and horns and a lonely death, and I thought about hopping into a cold shower, shock my senses to feel physical cues...drown away the mental anguish clutching me entirely.

A noise came from outside, someone shouting and pounding a door. I rushed to the curtains and peeped through a slit to see what was going on. Several motel rooms down on the adjacent row, Kimber was banging on a door.

He had my attention.

I situated myself in the curtains—a way to keep hidden but see out clearly. There was probably a younger woman behind that door, angry as a wet cat, all mascara tears.

The door flew open, and Jamie shot out, shirtless, jeans hanging low under his six-pack, and a half empty bottle of whiskey in his hand. "I can't do this tonight, Kims. Just go away." He tried to close the door, but Kimber stiff-armed it and pushed inward, both men in the doorway now.

"I don't give a shit!" Kimber yelled. But then he leaned closer to Jamie and his words went softer, and all I could manage to hear was tone. Something was going down for sure, but stepping out to try and calm them both down didn't seem like the kind of thing that would end up well for me. I was about to step back from the window when Kimber took off toward the parking lot, yelling back at Jamie as he walked, "You're going to fuck us! Get rid of it!" He slammed his truck door shut and peeled out, dust from the gravel lot kicking up, clouding his taillights as his tires squealed onto the paved road.

And then he was gone.

I looked back at Jamie's door, already closed. But he was in the group...he knew Dahlia and Ori and the itch to talk to him was tempting me to scratch. So very tempting; the worst idea. Shannon would be pissed.

***

"Hi," I smiled when Jamie opened the door.

His shook his head, confused, then his eyes went wide. "Johnna? What are you doing here?"

"I'm staying in room seven." I pointed over my shoulder to my door. "I heard the commotion and thought I'd come see how you were. I know how Kimber can be sometimes." I hoped throwing Kimber under the bus would break down Jamie's wall, or at least fracture it.

He sniffed, nose red from boozing all night. "He's just stressed about the business. It's not doing so good right now."

That could have passed as true, except, I couldn't figure out why Jamie was rooming at a motel when he and Kimber supposedly had a nice place together. Shannon talked it up pretty good, like they were swimming in money from the business their father had built. "I'm sorry to hear that business isn't good these days." I was buying time, thinking of how I could get him to open up more.

"I'm really tired, so uh...thanks for stopping by." He backed up to close the door.

I needed to get him to talk. "I've got some pills in my room."

The indentions on his brows lifted a bit. "Yeah?"

"Yup."

Then his eyes dropped to the ground. "Thanks, but I'm just going to hang back."

Kimber must have had him terrified. "Okay," I kicked at the moss growing between the cracks on the concrete walkway. The door started to close, and my mouth vomited words that my brain did not want it to. "Were you and Michael fighting over Dahlia? Did you hurt her?" *Fuck.* I took a deep breath, waiting for the Hager anger. I had no reason to say any of that other than to stir shit, hoping anger would fleet words from Jamie's mouth. Dahlia was gorgeous and jealousy was usually the spark that flamed rivalry between friends.

He stomped up to me, finger pointed, face red. "Your sister was a whore."

I couldn't take my eyes off the veins bulging in his neck, but I couldn't take my brain off what he'd just said. "Was a whore?" I took a few steps back. Poking the bear was not a good idea, but I needed answers and this kid had them. "I know you know something about her disappearance, Jamie...just fucking tell me!" I didn't want to yell, but it came out that way just the same and there we were, staring at each other like two deer in headlights, each of us afraid to make a move, and that told me more than he could imagine. He was just as afraid as me, only I didn't know what his trigger was. "I'm going to find out one way or another, Jamie."

He didn't look up at me, and I swear I saw him tear up just before the door slammed shut. What happened between him and Kimber to make him so afraid? What did he know about Ori?

The next morning, I drove by the Hager brothers' auto shop. Either Jamie was lying about business being bad, or an overnight miracle had struck with a slew of customers. As I passed, I saw Kimber in a blue one-piece coverall. He was standing underneath a lifted car, grease stained down to his elbows. Business seemed fine.

So, what the hell was the scream fest between him and Jamie last night really all about? I found a dirt road to turn around on and this time when I drove past, Kimber saw me, which wasn't exactly what I wanted, but I could come up with a reason for being out this way that wouldn't sound like I was spying on them. I was certain Jamie had told Kimber I stopped by his room last night. Kimber's stare was telling, and my skin pricked. His assumptions could be dangerous. The air went cold and suddenly I was very uncomfortable with him knowing my motel room number.

I pulled into the Piggly Wiggly parking lot. All I could smell was asphalt and the trash dumpster I'd parked too close to. The sun was full on and had dried up most of the storm's rain. I was choking on humidity.

Cool air hit my face when the building's electric doors whooshed open, the low melody of grocery store music lulling in the background. It was busy for noon; maybe because it was the middle of the month and the plant paid out its employees? In any case, there were only two cashiers and too many people in line for me to deal with after last night at Laurel's.

I debated my move, go in or leave. My mouth was dry, the heat outside zapping my fluids like a thirsty root ball. Nope...I was going in. "Goddamnit."

I walked the aisles, meandering a bit to give time for some of the customers to clear. Things like chow chow relish and pig snout weren't sold in the stores where I lived now; Northern Virginia was more organic breads and overpriced bottled water. But I'd grown up on this food and seeing it on the shelves was comforting. I made my way to the cooler section and grabbed some bottled waters and a Cherry Coke. Nothing tasted better after smoking than an ice-cold fruit-flavored soda. The cigarette line was still full, but I was in it now and I wanted a CBD cartridge. My weed was running out, and I needed to call in a refill on my meds.

The twenty-minute wait in line was worth it, the cold Coke rushing down my throat an immediate satisfaction once I'd snuffed my joint, dropped it in an empty prescription bottle and threw it in my console. I was properly awake now. I took out my phone and dialed Michael's number, hoping to get an answer. I didn't.

"Of course."

I called Laurel's number...no answer. "Jesus, why do they even have phones if they aren't going to answer them?" I took a deep breath. I'd been planning on ditching Laurel's because the thought of being in that house wedged a knot in my throat.

I wanted it to choke me.

Laurel's was a place of torment. My childhood died at the farmhouse, and now I was seeing things there. It made my stomach sick.

A knock on my window startled me, and I jerked my eyes to see Kimber standing outside my car, still in his work clothes, all wolf smile and intimidation. He'd have to do better than that to scare me though...or to see my *fear* anyway.

I turned down the window. "What's up?"

He yanked a red grease-cloth from his pocket and rubbed his hands clean with it. "You've got a flat."

What the fuck? I opened the door and stepped out. "No I..."

There it was, flat as roadkill on the yellow lines. "Shit." I bent down to look at it. "How in the world?"

Kimber joined me, nice cologne, sweat, and a hard day's work wafting from him like a fucked-up aphrodisiac. "Looks like you ran over a nail." He picked at the round, silver head lodged in my back left tire. "You must have run over it when you drove by the garage earlier." A tone, a look, the suspicion slipped from his mouth smooth as an eager tongue on bubblegum flavored lips.

I glared at him, then reeled that shit back in. "Hmm, yeah well doesn't matter where I got it." I stood and walked to the hatch. "It needs changing."

He stood. "I'll do it."

I shook my head. "That's okay. I've changed a flat tire before."

"It's my fault anyway. It's the least I can do." He whipped in front of me and opened the hatch.

Strange of him to claim it as his fault. "Yeah?"

"We really should keep a better eye out on the road for things like this. Don't want a lawsuit."

The hatch lifted, and I opened the cargo space where the tools should have been to replace my tire. "Where's my shit?"

"Did you forget to lock your doors last night? There're some sketchy people in and out of that motel you're staying at."

So Jamie did tell him I visited. "I do lock my doors." My heart raced. "Who the fuck broke into my vehicle without me knowing and took my shit? A professional mechanic maybe?"

He flashed a deviant smile. "I've got tools in my truck." He jogged the few parking spaces that separated our cars, and returned with a jack and crowbar, his forearms flexed by the tool's weight. He'd unbuttoned his coverall and pulled it down to his waist, a fitted black tank-top showing off the Hager family goods.

How were they all so perfect looking, like they were sculpted from clay and set to life. There was usually one sibling that took on the worst of the family genetics. I couldn't compare since Michael and Ori had a different father from me, but it was definitely a thing I noticed about siblings.

He bent to place the jack under the frame and a handmade beaded necklace popped out of his neckline, a charm of a black guitar pick dangling. "You still play?" I asked, trying to thin the air choking me.

He glanced down, shoved it back under his shirt. "A little."

I scanned the lot, shoppers here and there but all of them parked on the other side of the lot. The longer I stayed around Kimber the closer I came to panic. The fucking on and off button in my body had a mind of its own and it was flipped on now. I took deep breaths and let them out slowly, all while watching him loosen lug nuts at a snail's pace, time dragging its ass just to torture me. I wiped sweat off my forehead, tried calling Michael again...still no answer.

"Jesus," I mumbled under my breath.

"How's your ma?"

Like he cared. "She's fine. I—" I stopped myself from telling him that I was heading over there after the tire was fixed because I really didn't want him knowing my business.

"All done." He lowered the car.

Sweet relief. My muscles relaxed; I hadn't realized how tense I'd been. "Thanks." It was all I could do to not rush inside my SUV and lock the door.

He opened the door for me, and I wormed my way around him to sit inside. He leaned in once I'd fastened my seatbelt, his face too close to mine. "Did you really think talking to my brother was going to solve anything?"

My thoughts twisted up on each other. "I'm just trying to find Ori, Kimber."

"Stay away from Jamie." He pulled my seatbelt out and buckled it, pinning his body against mine. "You ain't gonna find your sister nowhere near him, you understand?"

I shrank, an uneasy feeling spinning itself into a fear tornado. He pulled himself out of the door and stood, watching from the darkest eyes. I fumbled to start the SUV, threw it into drive as soon as the engine kicked to life, and pulled away, watching him shrink as he stood around a pile of tools.

CHAPTER THIRTEEN

"Momma?" I called out. "The front door was open." I stepped inside, listened for the living room TV. A faint sound, mumbled voices, came from upstairs. Laurel's room.

I walked up the stairs, only thinking about Barrett for one brief second because my focus was on Laurel. "Knock knock," I said, at her door, which was halfway open. A squeak, the sound of old pipes shifting behind the walls. Laurel had just turned off the shower, so I went back downstairs to wait and see if she would come down. If not, I'd have to go back up.

Her bedroom door creaked open ten minutes later, the stairs cracking under her weight. She saw me at the kitchen table, her hair wrapped in a pink towel, a pair of loose joggers and a white T-shirt that once belonged to Barrett, too baggy to be Laurel's. "How long you been here?" she said, house shoes slapping the linoleum floor.

"Just long enough to make you a pot of coffee." I stood and went to the cabinet, pulled down a mug and filled it.

She sat at the table, expectant of my service, a droop to her face I hadn't seen in a long time. "Where are my cigarettes?"

Shit, I took them the other night. "I don't know. Michael might have taken them."

She hissed. "That boy wouldn't steal from me."

Only your money and your car and your food and everything. "Want me to go pick some up from the Pig?" The grocery store was a tad closer than the drug store.

"Nah, I've got a carton above the fridge up there." She pointed, as if I needed her to show me. I'd fetched them from there for her a hundred times. Stole them from there a million times, too. Guess Michael is the perfect child after all. I laughed to myself.

I placed the cigarettes on the table once I'd opened and packed them down for her. "I'm glad to see you're feeling better. I was getting worried about you."

She shrugged. "If this is better, I don't want to know what I was like before." The cigarette end crackled under the lighter's flame, Laurel relieved after flicking the wick a hundred times before a flame caught.

I kept thinking about the shadow upstairs, the image in the bathroom mirror. Maybe Laurel saw something too? The question bubbled up my throat and couldn't stop from asking. "Have you seen anything weird around here lately?"

Laurel hurriedly blew out a bloom of smoke. "What do you mean?"

"Like anything..." *Fuck me, she's gonna flip.* "Like a ghost?"

She shook her head, pointed a finger. "No, ma'am. Don't bring that Devil talk into this house." She slid her chair back and went to the fridge, pulled out a beer and gulped it like she hadn't had liquids in years. "You and your stories."

That was a direct reference to Barrett. She never believed anything I told her about him. Slapped me across the face once and dared me to speak of it again. So I didn't. Fucking bitch. "I think you had food poisoning."

She laughed. "Wouldn't be the first time. Haven't had a good meal since Barrett stopped cooking."

I was sick now. How dare she bring him up. But that was Laurel...all denial and narcissism. "Well, I've got to get back into town and buy a new tire, so if you're—"

"What happened to your tire?" Laurel flipped her ashes into the clean ashtray I'd washed last night.

"I ran over a nail." I realized I hadn't heard another sound from upstairs since I'd been there, which was strange because Laurel's car was outside, meaning Michael was there. "Where's Michael?"

Laurel flipped open a magazine and pretended to read it. "He's out at the barn working on his truck."

I stood and walked toward the front door.

"Where are you going?"

I tapped my pockets to make sure I hadn't put my keys down in the house. "To see Michael."

"Don't bother him with your problems. He's got enough of his own. Go to that garage down Route 9. Plenty of scrap shit out there."

I didn't want scrap shit. Scrap shit was the tire Kimber put on there. I could afford a new tire; I'd get a new tire, but I did want to see Michael. "He's my brother, Momma. I'm not bothering him."

"Johnna!" Laurel called after me, but I went out anyway.

I hadn't been to the barn in...well I couldn't remember. As I got closer, the single bulb drop-light shone brightly in my face as it hung off a long nail on the barn wall. Michael's truck was there, the front end completely gone.

I took in a deep breath, noticed the backwater stench and thought how out of place the smell was.

"What are you doing out here?" Michael's soft voice came from a dark stall.

I started to walk over, but he met me at the side of his truck. "Laurel told me you were out here."

He stabbed a shovel into the soft ground. "She told you to come out here?"

"Uh no. But I thought we could talk." I drew my eyes away from the shovel and to his, which were glossed over, as usual.

"What do you want to talk about?" He pushed past me and started circling the truck, picking up tools and wiping them down with a shop rag.

I didn't expect jerk mode to be activated so soon, and I hadn't even brought up the picture. "I don't know, Michael. Our sister is missing. Has been missing now for six days. I'm freaking out. I was hoping you would be too."

"If she wanted to run away, then let her."

"What makes you so sure she ran away, Michael?" I walked behind him as he tidied up.

"You ran away, and no one called in the FBI."

Asshole. "That was different, and you know it."

He sighed, dropped the wrench to his side and leaned against his truck, stray hairs from his man-bun sticking out like the electricity in those static balls. "I know. I'm sorry."

I leaned next to him and looked up at the rafters, noticed the rope we used to swing from was gone. "When did the rope come down?"

"It broke when Ori was swinging on it. She got knocked out. Mom made Barrett take it down that same day."

"Shame. I'd have hopped on it were it still here."

He huffed, a slight smile tugging once corner of his mouth. "You wouldn't."

"Yes, I would!"

He chuckled.

"Well, I need to go so I can buy a new tire."

He pushed back his loose hair. "Why happened to your tire?"

Kimber sabotaged it. "It got a nail in it."

"Don't go to Hager's." He bent over for another tool.

I eyed the shovel, noticed the fresh dirt on its spade. "I wasn't planning on it."

"Where are you going then?"

I didn't care about the tire anymore. "Hey, what were you digging?"

He glanced at the shovel. "A hole for that deer I hit."

The stench wafted. "Why does it smell like swamp in here?" I'd noticed the smell in the house before, but it was stronger now, and I immediately thought of Ori, only I wasn't sure why.

"What?" he bit.

I must have been having some weird kind of reaction to missing my Lexapro for two days. Seeing things, now smelling things. "It's nothing." This was the first decent conversation I'd had with Michael in forever, and bringing up a photo that likely meant nothing would ruin it. But Shannon was going to tell his boss. Michael deserved a heads-up. "Hey, there's something you need to know about." I wanted to cram the words back down my throat, let the stomach acid eat them until they were nothing but shit to be flushed.

"Mm, that doesn't sound good." He took the shovel up again, knocked dirt around with the spade's tip.

"I found your name written in rabbit blood on a stump by the old tree on Route 9."

His nose bunched up. "How do you know it's *my* name?"

"Because Ori had a picture of the skinned rabbit on her phone." Stared at his face, watching intently for that first sign of anger to flash in his eyes.

"I knew Dahlia was a bad influence on her. She was into to

all that bullshit because it's trendy." He let go of the shovel...let it smack the dirt as he walked away. "You didn't know her, but she was a little obsessive. I wasn't in love with her and that drove her crazy."

I stared down at the shovel, combing through scenarios. "So, she was doing a love spell?"

"Who the fuck knows." He was just outside the barn when he pulled out a cigarette. "She could have been trying to kill me." He pushed back his hair and flicked a lighter, his face a soft glow under the small flame.

I had no reason to believe Michael would kill anyone, but then again, I had every reason not to trust my family. "Shannon knows about it." Would this set him off?

My brother flicked ashes to the dirt and shrugged. "Good. Now he'll know how insane she was."

I walked closer, hoping he would stay calm. "And you had nothing to do with her murder?"

He laughed, tossed his head back and looked up at the sky. "Fucking Christ, Johnna. *I* didn't kill anyone."

I believed him, for whatever reason, and almost hugged him as I walked past but pulled back at the last moment. "Laurel seems better, so I'll be at the motel if you need me."

The Walmart tire center had to order my tire, so I was stuck with Kimber's freebie until tomorrow or the next day. I'd bought some grub from the local pizzeria and was comfortable in my motel room, ready to get back to finding clues about Ori. After stuffing my face with three pieces of meat lovers supreme, I grabbed the extra pillows off the spare bed and chucked them behind my head. I pulled out my phone—wanted to text Danae back since I'd ignored her call earlier.

I had to go back to North Carolina. Ori is missing. Don't know how long I'll be gone. I'll bring by your stuff when I get back.

She'd wanted us to get back together. She begged me to move back in. I tried to tell her it wasn't happening as well as I could, but she wasn't having it. I was a little on the fence myself, though I said nothing to her about it, but I sealed our break-up the night I fucked Shannon. There was no going back. Not for me.

Dusk fell fast, considering there wasn't a cloud in the sky all day, but another thunderstorm was coming. I wish it'd blow in news about Ori. I opened her social media again, went to her photos and scrolled through them for the hundredth time.

I stopped on a selfie of her lying in her bed, the family photo album open next to her. I zoomed in to see the photos inside the album. One of me and Michael playing at a lake. A distant memory that I couldn't retrieve fully. Another of the three of us at a Fourth of July parade, sparklers in hand, a sulfur smoke cloud blurring our faces. Since I was zoomed in, I moved the image around, analyzing the collection of mess on her bed. A seashell magnet from Myrtle Beach, a makeup compact from Sephora, the black and white striped bag lying next to it, and then I saw.

I sat straight up. "Holy shit." I tried to zoom in closer, but it wouldn't go any further. Lying next to an iPad was a fucking pregnancy test. I jumped up and put on my shoes, furious that Gabe lied to me. Pissed that Laurel and Michael couldn't care less, and God was I praying that if something had really happened to her, she wasn't with child.

Gabe had to know Ori thought she might be pregnant. That's probably what their fight was about. And Ori might have left to get an abortion safely away from him. Or something. I didn't know exactly what, but her disappearance just got a whole lot more suspicious, and Gabe knew more than he was saying.

My tires flung mud everywhere and though it was raining, I wasn't slowing down. My foot was heavy on the pedal, each second possibly getting me closer to answers.

At Gabe's house, I barely stopped before flying out of the car, running up on his porch and banging on his door like the house was on fire. "Gabe! Open the fucking door. I know you're home!"

Rain pelted me and the door, it was coming down in sheets. But still, he didn't answer. "I know about the pregnancy test!"

A few seconds later the door cracked open. "Come in."

My heart pounded in my temples. I had rushed over in such rage that I hadn't bothered to consider my own safety. If Gabe hurt Ori, nothing would stop him from trying to do the same to me. But I had to talk to him. I had to know if she was pregnant or if...*Or if Gabe even knew. Jesus fucking Christ, Johnna, just because she took a test doesn't mean Gabe knew anything, you idiot!*

I didn't bother wiping off my drenched shoes so they dripped all over his floor. "Did you know she thinks she might be pregnant?"

"She is pregnant."

At least I was right about something. "Holy fucking hell. Why didn't you tell me? Or the police?"

He snatched a throw blanket off the top of the couch, gave it to me. "So they could have more against me? No thanks."

I wiped down my face and arms, grateful for the gesture.

"They think you have something to do with her disappearance then?"

"I'm the boyfriend. We had a fight that night. Of course, they do. You do, too, don't you?"

I absolutely believed he could be responsible. Boyfriends are high on the list of guilty in these scenarios. But I had to keep my head straight. There was still Dahlia's murder, but so far, I couldn't connect Ori's disappearance to it. I certainly didn't have anything to tie Gabe to Dahlia. "Did you?"

He shakes his head in a disappointed laugh. "No, I didn't. I love Ori."

Again, I noticed he didn't say *loved*.

"It's not mine anyway."

"That's what ya'll were fighting about then, right?"

"Yeah."

I was going to be sick. I couldn't bear the thought of Ori going through something awful knowing she had a child inside her. She must have been afraid. "Well, whose is it?" I was terrified to hear his answer, my mind going straight to Kimber.

He shook his head. "I don't know."

"How do you know it isn't yours?" I tossed the blanket back to him.

A long sigh, a sad look. "I never said anything to anyone because this town is so fucking small and people talk too damn much, but I had an accident about a year ago at work. It made me sterile. I didn't say anything to Ori because we weren't at the stage of even talking about kids. She's supposed to be graduating high school for God's sake."

I turned the doorknob and open the front door. "You need to tell the police, or I will."

He shrugged. "Yeah, I will."

"Tomorrow, first thing."

"I got it. I know."

I slammed the door shut.

I was already halfway to Laurel's when I dialed Michael's cell.

"Hello?"

Hello? How did he not look at caller ID? "Michael, it's me. You still at home?"

"Yeah."

"I'm coming over. We need to talk."

"Okay." Then he hung up.

I tossed my phone into the seat, watched to see that it didn't slip between the crack, and when I looked back out at the road, someone was standing there; the same mangled shape I saw in Laurel's bathroom mirror. My mind had its own idea of who the shape belonged to.

Barrett.

I yanked the wheel, my mind conspiring against me, and threw my hands up to protect my face as a wide tree trunk barreled toward me. Images of Barrett's eyes—looking as they did when he would stare at me afterward—flew at me like some awful 3D movie. I'd been watching them zip past me when I saw the tree trunk speeding toward me. I threw up my hands to protect my face as my SUV plowed head-on.

CHAPTER FOURTEEN

I woke to a voice, deep and reassuringly familiar. "Johnna, can you hear me?"

It hurt to open my eyes, but when the blurry images of blue lights came into view, I saw Shannon. "What…"

"You were in an accident. Don't move." Sirens whirred in the distance.

"Are those for me?" I giggled. My reactions to trauma were something to be studied by psychologists.

"They are," he said, smooth…calm.

Louder and louder sirens echoed off the trees until finally they arrived, shut off the alarm and were at my car, prying me out with tools.

"Can you feel any pain?" a woman with blue-dyed hair and tattooed arms asked me. She was super-hot, and if I weren't dizzy and being pulled out of a car, I'd be blushing because her hands were all over my body. Like…everywhere.

I giggled again.

"Something funny?" she asked, genuinely amused.

"You're pretty." I smiled, groggy like some drunk awake too soon after passing out.

"Thanks." She continued working over my body, searching for injuries.

"I'm just a little dizzy. I don't think I'm hurt anywhere."

She looked at me squarely. "You have a gash in your head, but so far, that's all I can see. Once we get you out, we'll have to check for internal bleeding."

I took a deep breath. "My guts are fine." I smiled again. I knew I was okay. But the fact that I shouldn't be was drilling into the back of my brain.

At the hospital, I picked at the corner of adhesive in the bend of my elbow where an IV line was placed. I knew they would run a million tests because I had great health insurance.

A thin, middle-aged doctor popped into my room. "We can't find anything of concern, apart from the mild confusion. Other than that, you're fine," he said, pleased with himself in a way that played a little bit big...like *he* was why I was okay. He looked down at my arm and hand. "Oh, what happened here? Those injuries weren't from the accident."

"This one," I pointed to my finger, "was from a glass I was washing, and this one was from a rusty fence."

He gave me a serious look. "Are you up to date with your Tdap?"

Ugh, I knew that rusty fence was going to come back and bite me in the ass. "I don't know. Can't recall when I last had a tetanus shot."

"Better safe than sorry. I'll order the vaccine."

I rolled my shoulder back to stretch, my body stiffening from the wreck. "Can I go home after that?"

He didn't look up from the computer he was typing. "Well, I'd like to keep you overnight for observation, but—"

"I want to go home."

He looked at me over top his glasses, forehead bunched in

wrinkles. "I can't make you stay, Ms. LaGrange. But I'd like for you to at least get a tetanus shot."

Shannon's voice came from the doorway. "I'll take her home after her shot."

I craned my neck to see past the doctor and smiled, gave him a wink through a swollen eye. "My hero."

"I can turn on the heat for you," Shannon said, fingers reaching for the button in his car.

"No. It's hot as hell outside…I'll be fine."

"Here then." He reached into the backseat. "Put this on." He handed me his police jacket.

"Thanks." I put it on, tried not to inhale the smell of his cologne, but damn it smelled good, and nothing like Kimber's. I turned to look out the window, fog heavy from the mix of a hot day and an evening rain. I thought about the apparition in the road that made me crash…how it looked exactly like the body I saw in Laurel's bathroom mirror…how I thought it was Barrett.

My stomach flipped and bile crept up my throat. "Can you stop at the gas station? I need some water."

He turned into the parking lot, gently maneuvering his car around potholes. He didn't know I was nauseous but the whole concussion thing was probably running through his mind. "I'll go get it for you," he said, popping open his door before I could make a move for the handle.

"Thanks." I didn't mind the help. I didn't feel like walking into a halogen nightmare anyway. My head was pounding, and lights made it a hundred times worse. Even the glow that reached the car from inside the store was causing me to squint, so I reached in my purse and took out my sunglasses, placing them on my face like a shield from God.

He was in and out, the cold water a relief to my insides, to my thudding temples. "Ah...that hit the spot." I popped some acetaminophen and closed my eyes behind the glasses, resting my head on the passenger window.

"Don't you fall asleep, now, ya hear me?"

"I'm not. I'm just chillin'."

"Mm-hmm. You better not." He took my hand in his and rubbed his thumb over my knuckles." You going to the motel or..."

Was he asking if I wanted to go back to his place? A part of me did. I knew he'd watch me overnight. No one else would. But everything that had been happening to me happened at or near the farmhouse, so maybe if I went back, I'd see the apparition again. Maybe I could talk to it or reach out to it in some way. Find out who or what it was. Though...I might not like the answer. It could be Barrett. He did have a good reason to haunt me. I'd killed him after all. Well, shortened his fight at least. It was a losing battle. He was going to die regardless. "No. Can you take me to Laurel's?"

"Absolutely."

Our hands stayed interlocked until we pulled up to Laurel's and he needed to put the car in park. "Johnna...who in there is going to look out for you tonight? I can stay with you."

I leaned over, brushed my lips on his and gently pecked a kiss. "I would love to be with you tonight, but I think I just need to be alone...sort some shit out in my head, ya know?"

His hands lightly gripped both sides of my neck and he kissed me harder before pulling back. "I get it." The yellow porch light glinted in his eyes. "Call me tomorrow?"

I gathered my things and opened the door. "Yep." I smiled and stepped out. I leaned down to see him through the window. "Thanks...for everything."

He popped two fingers off his forehead in a salute. "My pleasure."

"You've been to Chick-fil-A too many times."

"I don't eat that shit." He laughed and put his truck in gear, drove off quietly.

I watched his taillights fade...wished I'd asked him to come in after all. I crept inside, didn't see Laurel or Michael, placed forty bucks on the kitchen table so that Laurel wouldn't bitch if she saw I slept over, and sluggishly walked up the stairs to Ori's bedroom.

Laurel must have cleaned up because the bedspread was gone. It had been a long day, and all I wanted to do was sleep, but the doctor ordered me to stay awake for at least three hours so maybe I could use that time to find out what had been following me. I kicked my shoes off and climbed into her bed, the soft mattress making it that much more difficult to stay upright. I sat with my back against the wall and waited...for anything to happen.

My phone vibrated and when I looked to see a text from my boss, it was 2a.m. I could sleep now. I slipped down, fluffed a pillow and closed my eyes.

My eyes flicked back open when something wet hit my cheek. I wiped it with my hand and brought it to my face...dirty water, smelling like swamp. I looked up at the ceiling.

An apparition hovered over me.

Inches away, spread the length of my body. It smelled like rot, slimy tendrils of grime hanging from its ears. Half its jaw missing—it was all I could focus on when it spoke. "Johnna," its voice like the popping of dried logs on a low fire.

Then it slammed down on top of me. I gasped when it hit.

A scream thrashed out of me, arms flailing to fight it, palms slapping against sinew and bone, fingers slipping and tearing through rotted flesh.

"Get off me!" I screamed. "Barrett! Get off me!"

I rolled off the bed and thudded to the floor, and when I looked back on the bed, it was gone.

I sat there, my body superglued to the floor, sweat stinging the million cuts from the wreck, every part of me afraid to move or make a sound. I didn't know what had just happened, but I still felt tension on my hands from when I pushed it off me.

"It's not real. Ghosts aren't real." Atheism was my moral center. Yet there I was, thinking that Barrett had broken my rules again and assaulted me from the underworld.

The longer I waited—eyes peeled like a barn owl perched on the rafters at night—the more I could convince myself that it was all my imagination. That I'd been under so much stress my mind had shattered, and when the pieces all landed, that horrifying shape was the mural they created.

Once my heart had snuggled down in its security blanket of normalcy, I pulled myself up using the fancy chair molding on the wall. Taking a step to see if I was ready to physically move, I exhaled, relieved I could walk without my knees buckling.

I snatched my things off the nightstand and trudged downstairs without a thought to what Laurel might ask if she saw me leaving. But the downstairs was dark, the kitchen empty...not even the blue glow of the TV. I was glad for that and didn't bother to leave a note.

Outside, I texted Alexis, Ori's former friend from the printing shop in town, and asked if she could pick me up. I didn't wait for her reply before I started walking toward town. One way or another, I was leaving the farmhouse tonight.

Ten minutes later, headlights approached, a car slowed, and when I saw Alexis's welcoming smile, I hopped inside her little green hatchback.

"I know this sounds clichéd, but you're a lifesaver." I tucked my purse on the floorboard between my feet.

A head tilt, the smack of lips. "Unfortunately, that's not the first time I've heard that."

She must have picked up Ori a hundred times, and I imagined Ori saying those exact words to her. "Folks like you are how cursed families survive." I smiled, but the truth of those words gripped my chest and my reflection in the window painted a clear picture of how awful it felt.

Alexis let out a heavy sigh. "Listen, I need to tell you something."

I perked, but her demeanor sagged, and her forehead creased. I recognized the shift in her. She was afraid. I'd spent most of my life being afraid, and there was no way of dealing except plowing straight through it. "I promise I'll keep your name off my tongue, Alexis. If you know something about Ori, please tell me."

She chewed her bottom lip, kept her eyes on the road. "Ori was fighting with Dahlia."

That's news to me. "Did Michael know?"

She shrugged. "I don't know."

"Okay, so what does this have to do with Ori going missing?

Her cheeks rose to the bottoms of her eyes, apprehension still puppeteering her. "Dahlia and Ori were fighting." She stopped abruptly, a sheen of tears glinting in her eyes.

Earlier though, she had said she wasn't close with Ori lately. So how would she know about the fight? "Who told you this? Are you sure it's true and not just 'town talk'?"

"Ori called me that night. She was crying. Said Jamie was cheating on her with Dahlia."

That made no sense. I'd just seen Dahlia's professions of love for Michael etched into her headboard. But someone wrote my brother's name on that stump. If it wasn't Dahlia then... "Ori," I mumbled. She must have done the love spell so Dahlia would fall back in love with Michael and she could have Jamie all to herself.

We passed Tantrums, Alexis's eyes darting over to the parking lot, Kimber's truck up front like a wart-tipped nose. Her breath hitched and she tensed. I wanted to push her, to get the information out of her that she'd almost given, but once she told me, she might never not be afraid, and I didn't want that for her. She deserved to feel safe, so we sat in silence until the motel.

"Thank you," I said, handing her a ten-dollar bill for gas.

"I don't want that." She smiled, and all I saw was her mother; it was as if Mrs. Brenda had spit Alexis right out of her mouth. "A ride is the least I can do."

"Oh, sweetie, please don't feel that way." My heart sank when I saw her eyes pool, her chin tremble.

"I feel so helpless." She wiped away a tear streaking her cheek.

"We all do. But listen, I'm organizing a search party of volunteers since the police are dragging their ass. I'll give you all the details when it's sorted."

"What do you mean the police won't do anything?"

I hung my head, trying to wrap their reasoning around my head. "They think she ran away."

"That's fucked up."

"Yep. But what can I do?"

She reached inside her purse. "I know what *I* can do."

My breath hitched. Was she going to tell me what she couldn't earlier? "Yeah?"

"My cousin is a reporter." She pulled out her phone and began texting. "A badass. She'll make the police get off their asses."

I perked. "Do I know her?"

"No. She's from Chicago, but she focuses on reporting about

police negligence. She worked that case of the missing soldier in California."

It took a second for me to recall, but then, "The young girl that vanished on base?"

"That's the one."

"Damn. Your cousin really is a badass."

Alexis smiled and flashed her phone screen at me. "Glad you think so. Her name is Shanique." She laid her phone on my leg and gestured that I take it. "She wants your number."

CHAPTER FIFTEEN

Xanax knocked me out for the next six hours. The room was dingy orange when I poked my head out from the covers despite the thick white curtains. All it took was the small crack I'd left in between them when I was spying on Jamie the other night. Might as well have had a discotheque in the room then. Concussions were a bitch.

I sat up, waited for the room to stop spinning before I found my phone and looked at the time.

"Shit."

Shannon had texted me so many times and the last one read, *Coming to check the motel.*

Serendipitous...his police truck pulled up just then. I didn't have to see it to know...just the way it sounded. And here I was still in yesterday's clothes. I jumped out of the bed, did a drive-by in the mirror to fix my hair and opened the door on his second knock.

"I'm alive," I said, nonchalantly, hoping he'd be chill. I didn't need the drama.

"I see." He gave me a once-over, sat his elbows back on his

equipment belt, a workday since he was in uniform. But he stayed silent, just breathing and looking at me.

"I'm sorry to make you worry." I wanted to be angry that he was so concerned, but there was a missing girl in his town, and I was that missing girl's sister...kind of seemed important that I keep him posted on my whereabouts...just in case. Besides, what if he's had a breakthrough and I wasn't answering my phone?

"Ah, I wasn't worried about you. If anyone can take care of themself, it's you." He turned to leave, obviously frustrated.

"Shannon..." He stopped and looked back. "Gabe said Ori is pregnant. And it isn't his."

His cheeks fell, a mumble of thought swallowed back down. "Well, that sure gives us a motive."

I'd come out of my room, was on the sidewalk. "Gabe isn't the only person we should be talking to."

"He's the only person we should be looking at. The only one with a reason to want her gone. He was either afraid she'd want to keep the baby, or he was pissed it wasn't his. Or both."

I held up my hand to block the sun. "What about Dahlia?"

His expression glitched, like I'd just slapped him. "What about her?"

Jesus, Shannon, I thought you were a good cop. "The girls were friends and now one is dead and one is missing. And now I know Dahlia was fighting with Jamie the night before she was murdered."

His hand flexed into a fist. "Who told you that?"

I wasn't ratting out Alexis. I threw my hand up in frustration. "I don't believe this. I thought you of all people would listen to me."

"Listen to you? What's that supposed to mean?"

I tossed my hair to one side, trying to block the sun. "I thought you would believe me when I tell you that in my gut, I think it could be someone else or that Gabe had help. That you would trust me." Gabe was not my lead suspect, but I was grasping at straws.

He huffed, lips clenched. "I was in love with you, and you left without a word. Why should I trust you?"

"Shannon," I reached out and took hold of his wrist, pulled him closer. "I dumped my girlfriend of two years because she proposed, and I couldn't give her what she wanted. I wasn't in love with her."

"What does that have to do with you leaving me?"

"You know that saying 'you can't love someone else if you don't love yourself'?"

He nodded.

"Well, it's a fucking lie. After Barrett did all those things to me for all those years, I hated myself. And I still hate myself, but I loved you."

"If you loved me then why did you ever leave?" His face drooped, desperate for an answer.

"I left here because everything I looked at reminded me of him. I couldn't bear it anymore, and you weren't ready to leave." I pulled him in, wrapped my arms around his neck and didn't stop him from picking me up and taking me into my room, laying me on the bed. He leaned in and kissed me again, a tug at the denim shorts covering my crotch. His finger slipped underneath my panties and pushed inside me...slipping out to rub the wetness on my clit. Another finger, faster and faster. "I want to taste you." He pulled his fingers out and stuck them in his mouth, lust drowning his cool demeanor.

I undressed him, he undressed me...our fingers eagerly searching each other. We kissed and nibbled and then I got up and asked him into a shower with me, steam dripping down the walls as I bent over for him to take me from behind. I grunted when he pushed inside me, his thighs slapping my ass as he thrusted. Harder, faster, deeper, his groans lodged in his throat.

I looked up at the white tiled shower wall, my palms flat against it, bracing his thrusts.

Water ran into my eyes and when I saw the dark slime oozing from the caulking, I brushed my face clear, but the walls still ran black. The shower stall filled with an unforgettable smell of sulfur and decay, a distinct scent of the marshes. I squeezed my eyes shut, he'd be done soon, and I didn't want my hallucination to ruin it for him. But the smell grew, rose, stirred in with the steam and laid on my skin like a cellophane wrap. A rock grew in my stomach, knocked back and forth like a ship in an angry ocean. Maybe a new equilibrium would jolt away the vision. I turned to face him and instead saw the corpse, flesh stained in death, and it opened its mouth, worms and water bugs rolling out, spilling onto the shower floor, a swirl of chocolate water taking some of them down the drain.

I screamed.

The corpse screamed back. I screamed harder, harder still until my throat went numb and nothing but fear wrapped in a whisper remained.

"Johnna!" Shannon shouted. He'd cut off the shower, was dripping wet, strands of hair stuck to his forehead. "What the fuck happened? Are you okay?"

Between gasps of air I said, "You didn't see that?"

"What?" He drew up his hands to cover himself as if someone were in the bathroom with us.

I guess not. "Never mind." I stood with his assistance, stepped out and wrapped a towel around me, handed him the other one. "I'm on a new medication. I think it's messing with my head a little, ya know with all that's going on and shit."

He shook his head. "I don't know what kind of medicine you're on, but if it's doing that you might want to let your doctor know."

I was lying under the covers, and he was putting on his last boot when he said, "I'm going to push motive for Gabe to the sheriff. We need to bring him in."

I took in a sharp breath through clenched teeth. Gabe wasn't the killer, only I had no way of proving it. It was just a feeling I had and couldn't explain.

"I'll see what the chief says." He stood up.

I rushed up to him, latched my arms around his neck. "I'm glad you're working this case, Shannon. I know you'll find her." My heart sank as an image of the police finding Ori dead crossed my mind.

He kissed me, lowered me until my bare feet hit the carpet. "I hope I don't disappoint you...lots of swamp out there."

His words poured over me like liquid nitrogen and I froze, choking on my own mind fuck as he walked out of my motel room. I took a sip of seltzer water. My stomach had been feeling extra icky ever since I hallucinated Barrett's corpse falling on top of me. I picked up the Xanax, broke the pill in half, but stopped short of tossing it back. I remembered Kimber and Jamie's fight. Kimber yelling for Jamie to get rid of something. But what? What could they be so angry about? Drugs? Money? Incriminating evidence?

My phone was dead, so I left it at the motel on a charger, but hopefully I wouldn't need it. I was in an Uber and thinking of the best place for the driver to drop me. I didn't want anyone to know where I was going, and once we made it to Route 9, the long stretch that connected the neighboring county, I asked the driver to pull over and let me out. It'd be a long walk back into town, but curiosity was a bitch and now was the perfect time.

"Thanks for the ride," I said, shutting the car door and stepping back. I watched until the Uber was gone and then took off through the small patch of woods that would dump me at the Hager's lot.

I walked to the back of the building, scanning the windows and doors. I didn't think they'd leave anything unlocked, but I tried the door anyway. At a window, I cupped my hands around my face to look inside...just a desk and some file cabinets. I didn't know what I was looking for or what I expected to find, but something tempted me here, I wasn't giving up until—

I picked up a tire iron that had been propped up against the wall, rusted but useful. I gripped it, flaking bits popping off onto the ground, and looked again at the window. If I triggered an alarm this would all be pointless.

How the hell was I going to get inside?

I walked to the fenced area where cars and scrap metal all blended into the dark trees behind the lot. I noticed a doggy door. "Great." But I had to get in even if it meant risking a bite from a mean old garbage hound. I dragged the tire iron across the chain-link fence and whistled. I waited for some rabid Saint Bernard to come lunging, teeth bared, foaming. But there was nothing. No Cujo in sight. Had the doggy door been an old addition that their father put in? I recalled a brown dog there when I was a kid, ears scabbed with insect bites. He was mean as hell...barked at anyone who stood outside the fence without one of the Hagers around.

Confident, or impatient, I climbed up and flopped my legs over, letting myself hang down before dropping to the ground on the other side. I was inside the fence, now I just needed to get inside the damn building. Goosebumps pricked my arms, and I longed for a hot shower, but a shower was a long way from here.

A low, throaty growl came from behind. I whipped around, a snarling big boy six feet away. Sneaky son-of-a-bitch. I white-knuckled the tire iron and slowly backed away, heart pounding. The dog wasn't up for my shit though; he lunged toward me. I spun around, bolted into a run for the nearest junk pile I could climb, an old military transport bus that had been in the lot since the beginning of time. I ran as fast as I could, blood pumping, throat clasped shut with fear; dogs were so much faster than humans...no way I'd outrun it.

I sped past a pile of car doors stacked one upon another, grabbed the top one and slung it to the ground behind me. It bought me just enough time to leap for the bus. Its doors were removed, the only thing to grab hold of was the large rectangular side mirror, but I'd have to toss the iron, and when it clunked to the ground, my heart did a summersault. I was weaponless.

I launched off the first stair with my shoe, gripped the metal anchor arm, and threw my leg up onto the hood. My other foot, still dangling, lit with fire as the dog nipped my ankle. I screamed, more terrified than hurt, dropped my other leg down, kicked at the mangey fucker until his bite loosened, a yelp echoing off the walls of stacked cars.

"Doesn't feel good, does it?" I taunted, pulling both my legs onto the hood, burning pain consuming my calf. Sitting on my ass, I pulled my ankle up to assess the bite. "Ugh." My stomach flipped, anticipation churning inside me. Good thing the dog was a wimp and didn't like being kicked in the head.

The junkyard was quiet, strange since a dog attack had just shot the night full of terror. But it was gone now, nowhere to be seen, retreated somewhere in the dark shadows cast by piles of stacked, crunched cars. My ankle lit with pain, the dog's teeth having raked across a mess of capillaries. I gripped the bottom of my T-shirt and pulled, ripping a piece off. Once it was tied, I stood on top of the bus hood, scanning the building from the higher viewpoint.

And that's when I saw a way in.

CHAPTER SIXTEEN

A small ventilation window was propped open just under the eave, but I couldn't reach it from the bus. I'd have to jump the gap onto the building's roof. Below, the dog circled the bus, determined to find a way to me. His bark was a siren I needed to silence, and the only way to do that was to disappear from his sight. I scanned the ground to see what was on the ground below in case I fell—nothing but an old coffee can filled with cigarette butts and five-gallon bucket of crushed beer cans.

I stretched, my fingers slipping through the grated window and sliding in to grip the inside. I leapt, ducking my head, my torso coming through, and there I was again with my legs dangling.

The opening was a little smaller than I anticipated. I was stuck. My palms went flat on the inside wall—cold, painted cinderblock—and I tried to wiggle through. Something was catching me at the waist. I thrust forward again, and still couldn't squeeze through. The metal button on my shorts was catching in the sill, pinching the skin at my belly button. I winced at the annoyance, used one hand to wrangle the button until it was free and then slipped through, falling ungracefully onto a tool table, the breath in my lungs forced out. I rolled off onto the floor, gulping for air my body couldn't gather.

"Ungh!" I gasped, writhing. I caught my breath and sat up, looking around the dark garage. Across the building was another room, door closed...a flaking stencil reading *office* was still legible. Maybe the Hagers had secrets behind that closed door.

I walked, knees shaking, across the three-bay shop, a large vehicle covered in a tarp, another car still lifted in the air above a mechanic's pit. I wasn't sure if the elevated car meant someone was coming back soon to finish the job or not, so I needed to get moving if I didn't want to get caught.

The office door opened with a twist of the knob. If only getting inside the building had been that easy. I felt a pull, the urge to go inside the office further, to the desk. As if I had an unknown piloting system directing me.

A messy pile of invoices and receipts and manila folders strewn about without purpose. But just as my fingers touched down on a stack of files, they slipped past and went to the bottom drawer, as if guided. I pulled the handle, it didn't budge. "Shit." Must be something important in this drawer for the Hagers to keep it locked. In the movies, the thief always pulled out a pin from their hair to jiggle the lock open. But real life was much more difficult, so I figured this would be too.

I went back out into the shop, searching for anything that might resemble a wedge. Nothing. I thought about the tire iron outside, but the trip in and out of that window was one-way, which reminded me that I was going to have to figure a way out once I was finished searching for whatever I was there for.

Squatting in front of the desk drawer, still no idea how to get in, I slipped my fingers around the handle and pulled as hard as I could, and the more the drawer resisted the angrier I got, like the contents were the answer to everything wrong in my life.

Tears stung my eyes; I couldn't explain why emotions were boiling. I was a teenager all over again...all tempered to rage.

A loud pop, my ass falling back onto the floor in a painful thud. But the drawer was open now and my heart raced to see inside. I shot up, ignoring the pain in my tailbone from hitting the concert floor. My hands couldn't file through the contents quick enough. A half empty bottle of cheap whiskey; a somewhat creased white T-shirt; three packs of Marlboro cigarettes...a letter-sized envelope taped closed.

I struggled to lift it out, the liquor bottle clanking loudly, but now the envelope was in my hands and discretion flew out the window. I ripped it open, dug my fingers inside and retrieved the papers...the lease to the garage the Hager brothers inherited from their father when he died.

"Fuck." I slumped back, my ankle burning, the dog bite wound bleeding through. All of this was for nothing. Why did I have the urge to stop here...the absolute certainty that something was in that drawer? I slammed the drawer shut, my hands shaking. I didn't want to think about having to break out of this place...and empty-handed to boot.

Fuck that. I went back out to the bay, scanned the large space for...anything. My eyes landed back on the covered car. It wasn't out of the ordinary to see a tarped car in a shop, right? I stared at it, my head tilting in thought, and the longer I stared the more I wanted to pull off the cover.

So I did.

And there was Ori's car.

A million hammers beat inside my chest. Why was her car here? Was she having it worked on before she went missing? How come no one mentioned that to me? Shannon had to know Ori's car was there.

I threw open the driver door—the smell of old nicotine and weed hitting me in the face—crawled inside and began rummaging like the criminal I had become. I flipped open the console, picked through a chewing gum packets, strawberry lemonade body spray, but nothing revelatory. In her glove box was more of the same, a few drive-thru fast-food receipts, and unopened cigarettes boxes.

I stood up, cupped my sore ass, and shut the car door, not paying attention to my surroundings.

"Hey!" a voice shouted.

It only took a second to recognize Kimber's voice. I spun around, flinched at the sight of him, metal pipe tucked to his side.

"Shit, Johnna." He stepped closer. "You just don't listen."

"I was looking for clues."

Kimber's expression twisted, wrinkles in his forehead pushed down his eyebrows. "And you think you found one?" He motioned to Ori's car.

"Is it?" I backed around Ori's car with each step he moved closer. It was a dance of cat and mouse, and I was the tiniest mouse in a lion's cage.

His eyes narrowed as he moved to block me on the other side. "Of course, you think the mean ol' Hager brothers got your sissy."

The way his voice hissed out *sissy* sent me to rage. "That's her car isn't it?" My tone was slick venom.

He nodded. "Oh, it's hers alright. Perfumed in whore and bubblegum."

I knew it when I saw that picture of him and Ori shot gunning that joint...Kimber wanted her, and she dissed him, just like I had dissed him, and he hated both of us for it. "What did you do to her?"

He laughed, almost gagged on his own spit. "Me?" He put his hand to his chest as if I'd offended him. He was close enough that I couldn't move anywhere now that he couldn't reach. It was me wedged between two walls of cinderblock and no way out.

Kimber lifted the pipe, stretched it out to keep me wrangled as he stepped inside my space. "I thought I was done with you bitches." In his free hand, the dull blade of a weathered hunting knife tipped toward me. "My life is about to get a whole lot easier."

His image blurred before me as tears pulled my eyes. It was hopeless; all I could do was lunge for him, try to catch him off balance. But as I propelled forward, he reacted faster, stepped aside and swung the pipe around my neck, pulling my back against his chest. With each breath I tried to take, the pipe dug deeper.

"Just let it happen, Johnna. I'm not going to prison for ya'll bitches." Kimber bit, tucking the pipe into his elbow and squeezing tighter.

If I just let it happen, then Ori's killer goes free and the thought of him hurting someone else...

I reached my hands up to his face, digging my nails into his skin and pulling down. If he killed me at least the cops could find his DNA on me.

"Ugh!" He screamed, pulling back a little. Not enough. I gasped, the last of the air in my chest rushing out. White light flashed in my vision, a high-pitched hiss in my ears. All I could think about was if Barrett felt this same exact way while I was killing him.

I smiled.

———

My body was weightless, the world muffled. I flicked open my eyes to a wet darkness, unable to see when clouds covered the full moon. It was like looking through a dirty window out into the night. I screamed, water rushed in, and I coughed out all my air. My limbs flailed, a seatbelt across my chest trapping me, my hand bounced off a steering wheel. *I'm submerged. In a car.*

A glint of silver caught my eye, a lanyard with 2023 *Graduate* hung from the rearview mirror. My heart sank. Ori was supposed to graduate that year. I fidgeted for the release and when the seatbelt loosened, I kicked, praying like hell that the window was down. But my hands smacked against glass, so I pivoted and started kicking the window with my feet. At first, my feet bounced off, knees almost hitting me in the face, but I kept kicking until the glass shattered. I squirmed through the opening, shards cutting me on my hands and arms as I gripped the frame to propel myself out of the car.

Once freed, I kicked and paddled and prayed that I was swimming upward. My lungs burned to breathe, the urge becoming impossible to fight. I kept my fingers tight together, kicked so hard my shoes popped off, but the surface wasn't coming. I was about to lose, to fall back down below the dark water, sink until I hit bottom, and there was where I'd die.

And here it came, the battle lost. My mouth opened to inhale.

I devoured the air as I broke the surface just then. A long, gasping sound lurched out of my mouth, and my arms thrashed to find the balance that would keep me afloat. I coughed up water that had made its way into my lungs, the taste muddy river water familiar.

A current caught me, but it was calm, so I rode it downstream as I struggled to swim for the bank. A light ahead, the soft sound of a boat motor. I flailed my arms. "Help!"

A spotlight bounced across the water's surface until it found me. I waved my arms. "Over here!"

"Holy shit." The fisherman's voice was wet and croupy, the voice of an old man who spent a lifetime sucking on unfiltered cigarettes. The boat drove closer, a life jacket splashed the water in front of me. "Take hold of it."

I did. Gripped it like it were my soul trying to leave me.

"Grab my hand." The fisherman leaned over, a long, sturdy arm for me to hold on to. He lifted me into the boat, brown algae slipping off my skin and slithering back into the water. "What the fuck you doin' out here, girl?"

I didn't answer, only took in deliberate breaths, concentrating on living. "I fell in," I said, finally.

"No shit. Where at? What happened?"

No clue. But I wasn't explaining it to Long John Silver. "I was stupid, got too close and slipped on mud."

"You camping out here somewhere? You fucking tourists. Always getting yourselves in trouble around here."

Joke's on you...I'm a local. "Yeah...sorry about that." I sat up, saw a phone at his ear.

"Yeah, I just pulled a lady out the water down here just past Wilford's Cliff. She needs medical attention."

No, I don't. "I'm fine." I needed to get my story straight because this was going to be wild, and Shannon was going to flip. I had no explanation of how I got in Ori's car that had been submerged in the river. I couldn't explain why I didn't drown. There was no way to make sense out of any of it. Either I was insane and none of this was happening, or something supernatural was going on. I took another breath, trying not to vomit. "And tell them I found Ori Kern's car."

CHAPTER SEVENTEEN

Emergency response vehicles and news vans littered the riverbank, red and blue lights strobed the forest, and in those moments of flashing bright and blinding dark were images of blood and hair and teeth. I blinked and rubbed my eyes, but the images wouldn't stop. So, I closed my eyes, trying to see them more clearly. If they kept bombarding me then maybe I needed to be seeing them?

Shards of glass glinted in the night, a bright light nearby illuminating them. Screams, shrill...guttural, cut through a blaring car horn.

I opened my eyes and looked down at my hands now, small cuts from the shattered glass car window burning with river water.

Flash. Flash. Flash.

A blurry tree line, the stench of swamp.

My eyes were still open; the vision came through still. I turned away from the forest, afraid I'd see something staring back at me. A dull white tinged the horizon, dawn overcast in gray from yet another summer storm. It had to be a record of some sort, the amount it had rained just since I had arrived was astronomical.

I rubbed my fingers together, the tips pruned from being underwater. But I couldn't have been under long enough for my skin to become waterlogged, or I would have drowned. Nothing made sense and I couldn't stop crying. How was I supposed to tell the police what happened?

A medic gave me a hot coffee, and I pulled the blanket tighter, watching the scene from the hood of Shannon's police truck as divers searched for Ori's car. When I saw Shannon walking over after speaking with the fisherman, my stomach coiled in on itself.

"How bad are those cuts?" His brows dipped, wrinkles lining his forehead.

I popped an arm out of the blanket. "They're fine. Just needed some ointment and bandages." I stuck my hand back inside the blanket when he reached for it. It was bad, needed stitches, and I wasn't about to show him the dog bite even though a medic dressed the wound. But I wasn't leaving until they found my sister's car. I needed to know that it wasn't a dream. And if it wasn't, this town was too small for no one not to know something about this.

He leaned next to me on the car. "Johnna, what the hell were you doing down here so late...and alone?" He kept his eyes on the search party, boat lights glaring off the water's surface.

"Shannon"—I gripped the hot coffee and brought it to my chest—"I need to tell you something."

He hugged me, wiped a falling tear off my cheek. "It's okay. You're safe."

His hug was so reassuring. I knew if anyone would believe me, it would be him. "I fell asleep in my bed last night and the next thing I know, I'm waking up under water. I—" I choked, let tears spill until there were none left. "I'm so scared."

He squeezed me tighter. "We'll find out who did this to you."

I bit back Kimber's name before it had a chance to live. Honestly, I wasn't sure Shannon would believe me if I told him the truth...that his own brother tried to kill me. But it wasn't me that needed a voice, it was Ori, and Kimber needed to pay for what he'd done to her and Dahlia.

Shannon took my hand and inspected it, giving me a side-eye. "These need more than ointments and bandages. Look"— he lifted my arm— "they are bleeding through." He scanned for help. "Hey." He caught an EMT's attention and waved them over.

My coffee sloshed around the disposable cup's eyes, my hands still trembling. "Shannon...I need—"

"We'll get a blood sample from you. If someone drugged you, it'll show up. Until then, I'm not leaving you alone."

"No one drugged me," I said through a sniffle, and took another sip of coffee, its aroma snuffed by river debris still lodged in my nose.

He shuffled to face me. "What do you mean? How do you—"

Just say it. I lifted my teeth off my tongue. "It was Kimber." There. It was out now. Like a Band-Aid ripped off a nasty wound, the gaping hole left exposed and vulnerable.

He stared at me...flatlined expression. It was like I'd hit his pause button. "Say something," I whimpered, mouth hovering above the rim of my cup, like the coffee was my comfort blanket. His silence was making me nervous. He didn't believe me. I remembered scratching Kimber's face and held out my hands to examine underneath my fingernails. "I tore his face up pretty good before he choked me out."

Shannon glanced at my hands, a hodgepodge of dirt and cuts spread over them. The crunch of foot beats sent our attention to the approaching medic, and Shannon took both my hands and held them up. "Get forensics to swab under her nails for possible evidence before you bandage them." He dropped his hands and mine stayed in the air, the medic gauging the wounds.

"Sure thing," the medic said, dropping a tote bag to the ground.

Shannon started to walk away.

"Where are you going?" My voice cracked and I coughed, and dank river water piped up my throat. I gagged and tried to choke it back down, coughing and gasping for air, and by the time I caught my breath, Shannon was tearing away from the scene, his truck tires flinging mud and debris. He was going after Kimber, and I had no choice but to deal with bright headlamps and wet swab sticks.

That's when I heard "We found it!" blast from the nearest firefighter's walkie.

I jumped up. I needed to see it for myself." I slapped away the helping hands and walked toward the shore, the divers' heads bobbing, daylight barely breaking, but it was enough to see the search zone, the crane's line disappearing below the surface, ripples fanning out as the car began to break the surface.

And there it was. A fender, a tire, the rim spray-painted hot pink because that's who Ori was. A hot pink wonder seeking thrills and finding trouble. The back quarter panel, still shining with its factory black paint. And then...the license plate, *WLD-CHLD*.

I grabbed my temples and squeezed, as if that would erase everything.

The crane still had Ori's Hyundai dangling like some prized fish, and I ran for a nearby tree, buckled and puked, the taste of coffee stinging the back of my throat. I wiped my mouth and went back to the riverbank, sat my ass on a piece of old wood. My stomach had all it could take for one day. I dropped my head to my hands unable to process what was happening.

"We've got a body!" an agent yelled, his hand still on the hood of the opened trunk.

The world slowed as I searched for the sheriff. His mouth was moving, but I couldn't hear what he said, like he was behind a wall, and I was on the other side. My mouth went dry; I swallowed, a golf ball of dread grated my throat. I wanted my feet to move, to walk me over to the car so I could see, but they didn't budge. Shaking began in my knees and ribs, then consumed me completely and no amount of mylar blankets could warm me.

I knew it was her. I'd just found my sister's body. The whole time I'd been in Sweetwater, she'd been stuffed in the trunk of her own car, all alone, like a forgotten gym bag. And Kimber put her there. My eyes blurred, a fist of heat expanding in my stomach. He killed my pregnant sister, then put us both at the bottom of this "Fucking river!" I screamed, dropping to my knees and sobbing in my hands.

Someone knelt next to me, cupped their arms around me and held me while I cried. I didn't know how much time had passed between then and when another agent's words backhanded me. "It's not her!"

Everything around me went still, the dizzying emergency lights, the rushing waters against the bank, boat motors, voices of so many people...it all stopped. My ears rang, high-pitched and ready to burst.

"It's not the Kern girl," I heard someone say.

"Huh," I muttered, trying to stand, and when a helping hand reached for me, I looked to see the medic beside me. "Thank you." I said through a glob of snot and tears. I turned my eyes to Ori's car, murky river water still bleeding out the door seals. "Who is it, then?"

The medic shook her head. "I don't think they know yet."

My legs wobbled as I walked closer, the medic's arm catching my shoulder. "Miss LaGrange, you don't want to see what's in that trunk."

I stopped, stared at her car. "Are they sure it isn't her?"

She shouted to the search and rescue agent. "Hey, does she need to confirm?"

"No. It's a male," they shouted back.

She turned me away, gently. "You don't need to see."

I almost complied, but I needed to know if the horrific corpse I'd been seeing looked like what was in the back of that car. "I have to."

Debris cracked under my feet as I walked closer, leaves, twigs, small pebbles, and the bare skin of my soles flinched with every step. I guess I'd gone soft living in the city for the last ten years, but when I was a kid, my feet could walk over broken glass and I wouldn't have felt a thing.

I was at the trunk, just a peek away from seeing.

I inhaled sharp and quick, the corpse staring at nothing, eyes milky blue, skin slick with river sludge. "Jamie?" I muttered, the back of my hand on my lips, stifling an urge to puke.

CHAPTER EIGHTEEN

We approached the interrogation room at the station, heard a mangle of voices behind the door and before I was ready, the sheriff pushed it open. "This way," he said, his tone as close to comforting as it could be considering no amount of sugar could fix this. I wasn't ready for the eyes, a set of six blinking back at me, expectant, judgmental...curious.

"Have a seat, Ms. LaGrange." The sheriff motioned to a vacant chair. I sat, wiping sweaty palms on my pants. I looked like someone they'd just pulled off the streets, still wearing the clothes they saw me in last night, sans bra. "You can call me Johnna, Sheriff Locklear. You've known me since I was a baby."

"Ms. LaGrange, how did you find your sister's car?" Each of the agents shuffled in their seats, except the one standing behind me leaning against the wall. She kept popping her gum.

My chin trembled. I'd already told the police what happened, but this was formal and FBI were investigating now. "Kimber Hager attacked me. When I woke up, I was in Ori's car." Tears pooled; my vision blurred. I broke then, shoving my face into my hands.

The sheriff cleared his throat. "We've got a team out looking for him. And Officer Hager," he added. "When was the last time you saw Jamie?"

I sniffed, sucking up nose drips. "The other night at the motel I'm staying in."

"Do you know anyone who wanted to hurt Jamie?" He adjusted his pants at the waist, shuffled himself to realign his uniform.

"No. I just got here a few days ago." I looked around for tissues but saw none.

His eyes darted to the other detectives. "What was the circumstances of you seeing Jamie last?"

Oh shit, I hadn't thought about that night, how angry Kimber was. "I was inside my motel room and heard a shouting outside. When I looked out of my window, I saw Kimber and Jamie yelling at each other, and then Kimber peeled out of the parking lot." Kimber did this; I wanted them to catch his ass... before Shannon. "He yelled at Jamie saying Jamie was going to fuck them. I don't know what that meant."

The sheriff nodded. "Did you speak with Jamie that night?"

Yes. "No. I stayed in my room." The lie came out so easily. I prayed the cheap motel didn't have surveillance outside.

He scribbled on the notepad in his hand. "Have you had any correspondence with Ori since she disappeared?" That one pissed me off. I could have punched him on the nose, made it redder and shinier than it was now; his effort at hiding his drinking was less than professional. Even Laurel could hide it when she wanted, and she was a mess.

"No, sir. I'm down here looking for her in case you missed that part." My sarcasm didn't fall on deaf ears.

He huffed a coy laugh. "No, I know you came here from the city."

Again, with the city shit. These fucking people. "It's not—" Never mind. "Can I go now?"

He looked around the room for approval. The agents nodded in agreement. "We're going to keep a patrol car outside of your motel room. You'll be safe."

There was a deluge of uncomfortable throat clearing in the room. "Ms. Kern needs to be notified. The department is preparing to put a massive search party together. We're doing everything we have in our power to find your sister."

Swallowing a world of despair down, I said, "No, I know. I'll tell Laurel." I stood, looked at the men. "Is there anything else you need from me?"

"Don't leave town." He looked at me, bushy brows creeping over his eyelids.

With all that had been going on, I hadn't had a minute to actually organize a search. I didn't even know where to begin. But I was relieved that the police were going to search now. It would keep them occupied while I kept investigating on my own. "I wasn't planning on it," I snipped.

The sheriff stood, put his hand on my back and ushered me gently to the door. "We're going to find her." He sounded as confident as a dead-beat on the stand defending all the reasons why they needed yet another chance.

I thought of Michael's girlfriend. "Like how you found Dahlia? Do y'all even have a suspect yet?"

His cheeks flushed red. "We are doing everything we can. Don't think for one second otherwise."

I walked through the open door, kept my head down, wrapped my arms around myself because fuck...I needed some kind of comfort. The sheriff was ushering me out through the main entrance where a group of police and detectives were gathered—swapping stories about last night—and then Gabe Ingle walked through the doors.

I was ushered out of the station quickly; I couldn't get a word in with Gabe. I'd have to wait to hear from the detective about his statement. He could still be a suspect in Ori's case. Ties ran deep in Sweetwater, and I had no way of knowing if Gabe was tangled with the Hager boys.

The officer took me to the farmhouse. I didn't want to be alone at the motel. It was sad when Laurel's company was better than my own. The police car rolled up to the farmhouse, a news van already set up, the reporter hitting on a vape while scrolling through her phone, a cool lean against the porch stair railing. I had to admit, she was ballsy, her black Louboutin heels propped against the under-siding.

"This is private property." The officer begrudged her, slamming his car door. He turned to me. "The press shouldn't be here."

I looked down at my clothes, pushed my hand through my hair. "It's fine. I don't mind talking to them. I kind of got used to it in my line of work."

He looked at my clothes. "Do you want the world seeing you like this?"

I couldn't even remember if I'd brushed my teeth for that matter. "No, but word needs to get out and I can't think of a better way."

The reporter kicked off the banister, licked her glossed lips, dark brown eyes squinting when she smiled. She walked toward us, pulling out a business card, polished nails clicking on the cards' carrying case. She handed it directly to me. "My name is Shanique Rollins. The reporter from Chicago...Alexis's cousin."

It took a second to recall, but she saw my expression change the moment I remembered and continued. "I promise to cover this story with care...tread delicately." Her eyes softened, a serious and sincere expression. "I know how small towns work. I don't want to make this clickbait or any of that bullshit."

She was telling the truth. How could anyone wear a face like that while lying? Besides, I was stupidly gullible for pretty girls. "Thank you, Shanique."

She asked the same questions as the police, and I answered them truthfully, except on how I found Ori's car. I didn't mention Kimber and when the officer noticed I was deflecting, he nodded in agreement. After the questioning, her personality zipped up smooth like a Coach purse, swift and precise. She was done with me. She popped her hip when she turned away, her only worry was getting the story, and she'd just sealed the deal.

"You know her?" The officer watched the reporter until she was in her rental and driving away, paper company plates flapping in the wind.

"No." I choked; the reality of Ori likely being dead swelled inside.

I stayed on the front porch, sitting on the top step, letting the sun warm me. I could land on its surface and still never find warmth again. I'd called Michael from Laurel's cell; she was still sleeping, and knew he'd be there soon, but Shannon was still MIA, and I was worried he'd found Kimber. I needed my phone. The grind of tires over crusting mud drew my eyes to the driveway where Michael pulled up. I limped down the stairs, hopped inside the car and tried not to cry.

His face was pure confusion. "Okay, I guess we are going somewhere?"

I wiped my face with the palm of my hand. "I'm checking out of the motel."

He raised an eyebrow. "Are you leaving town?"

I wanted to say yes, but I had to find Ori. And Shannon

needed me. Plus, my SUV was totaled. So many things were keeping me there. I felt more locked to this town now than I ever had before. And it made me sick. "No. I'm staying a little while longer."

The town was getting closer as I procrastinated telling Michael the news. My throat was sore from screaming and crying and to know Michael would be feeling all that sent a fist to my heart. But putting it off wouldn't help. "Michael, they found Ori's car." There, I dug my fingers nails under and ripped off the scab. "It was at the bottom of the Cape." Vomit acid burned my throat.

When he didn't vocalize, I turned to him.

"Hey," I said. "Did you hear—"

He snatched his phone from the console. "I heard you." His fingers tapped at the screen, eyes looking away from the road. He presumably sent a text, clutching the phone in his fist as he drove, his bottom lip getting the chewing of its life.

I tried to read him, but Michael was like a reptile, all dead-eye stare and vacant. "Did you text Laurel?"

"What?" He turned to me. "Uh, yeah I texted Mom."

We pulled into the motel lot, Jamie's vehicle sitting there. I avoided it like it were a contagion. "I'm going to shower and grab my things. I promise I'll be quick."

He nodded and took out a cigarette.

"Don't leave." I needed him to promise he wouldn't.

His eyes bugged out, and he blew a puff of smoke at me. "I'm not going to leave you. Go."

In the room, I snatched my phone and texted Shannon and when he hadn't responded after my shower, I called.

No answer.

Back in the car, I rifled through my bag searching for my charger. My hands shook. They might never still again. "You got a charger in here? I can't find mine."

Michael pointed to the console, and I opened it, noticed some empty mini bottles and a half burned joint. I reached for it. "This is exactly what I need right now."

He looked over. "No!" and snatched it away. "This will fuck you up like you've never been fucked up before."

"That's kind of the point."

"Here." He leaned across me, opened the glove box and pulled out a ziplock bag. "You'll like these better."

I opened the bag, pulled one of the many joints out. "If that's not prepared, I don't know what is." I lit it, took a long drag and didn't pass. My feet were cold, so I put them on the dashboard where the heat I'd turned on against Michael's will could warm them.

He eyed my feet in repulsion of the heat. "I offered my flannel."

"Thanks, but your clothes smell like cigarette smoke."

He nodded, kept his eyes on the road. "You smell like weed."

I laughed, a plume of smoke blew out of my mouth and swirled around the air vents. But my smiled faded. "There's more I have to tell you."

"Yeah?"

I took another drag and blew it out slowly, hoping the world would end before I had to tell my baby brother that the police found Jamie in Ori's trunk. I shook my foot faster and faster until Michael looked over at me.

"Can you stop that? You're shaking the whole car."

I dove in. "They found Jamie in the trunk." Kimber trying to kill me had to wait. Michael was delicate; I couldn't put all of it on him. He might run off and never come back.

When he didn't respond I faced him, his jaw clicking so tight I thought I heard his teeth crack.

"Michael?"

"That can't be true." His fingers stretched, readjusting his grip on the steering wheel.

"It's true, Michael."

He went silent again...and then he hit the brakes and we slid to an abrupt, squealing stop. "FUCK!" he screamed, and I didn't think he'd ever stop.

CHAPTER NINETEEN

Michael took my bags inside for me. I'd asked him to set me up in Ori's room, and I was surprised he'd only given me a side-eye, much like the one he shot at me as he lugged my suitcase upstairs. The house was obnoxiously quiet, my skin pricking with caution, a side-effect of growing up in a home that wasn't safe for any child. Strange how only just now I'd made the correlation between the house being quiet and being alone with Barrett.

"Momma?" I called through the kitchen and into the living room, noticing the kitchen table was clear of its usual littering... shot glass, ash tray, an old iPad propped open, screen streaked with fingerprints. When she didn't respond, I walked on into the living room. Nothing in there but dust and the throw blanket I'd given her days before. "She must be in her room."

"She is," Michael said, standing in the door frame, looking blankly at the television that wasn't turned on.

"Is she okay?" This wasn't normal Laurel behavior.

He shrugged. "I don't know how she could be."

Irritating reply. "Well, is she in her room?" I pushed past

him and made my way upstairs, irritated that he followed me. "You should have told me she was still sick, Michael," I whispered over my shoulder at him.

"I didn't know she was."

It sounded so much like the truth that my brain twisted, and I couldn't think straight. I knocked on her bedroom door. "Momma?" When she didn't answer I went inside, orange evening light casting through red sheer curtains, and there she was, clammy, pale, eyes open. I rushed to her bed. "Momma. Are you okay?" I shook her gently and she stirred, her eyes flapping closed and my heart flipping on its end. "Jesus," I gasped.

I stood up, turned to Michael. "Is she on drugs?"

His lips turned down and he shoved his hands in his Dickies. "I don't know. Probably."

I shook my head. "Probably?" This was the last thing I needed. "She's probably having a rebound from the virus. They do that sometimes."

"If you say so. Want me to get her some medicine from the bathroom cabinet?"

"Yeah, and a wet washcloth."

I reached down, lifted Laurel onto her pillow because no one deserved to wake up with a kink in their neck from sleeping wrong all night. She swatted at me, mumbled under her breath. "Come on, Momma. I'm just trying to help." Her eyes rolled alive, wide, focused. "Are you okay?'

"I..." she croaked on the drought in her mouth. "I'm fine."

Michael returned with a plastic dosing cup full of the nasty green. "You don't look fine, Momma." He tried to hand it to me, but I stepped aside so that he would have to give it to her. "Michael has some medicine for you to drink."

She tossed it back like a shot of vodka, flashed a squinty sideways glare at us. "What are y'all both doing here?"

I grit my teeth, wanted to turn around and walk out, leave her there with the sticky taste of hot medicine in her throat. But instead, "We came to check on you." I lifted an empty glass off her nightstand and went into the bathroom to refill it.

Michael gave me a curious look when I returned, mouthing, "Are we going to tell her?"

I shook my head; now was not the time. "I'm staying here now, Momma. If that's okay?"

Laurel smiled, twisted and not at all sincere. "You gonna give me some rent money. You're too old to be living at home for free."

I shot a glance at Michael, the golden son of twenty-four years who never gave Laurel a dime. "Yeah, Momma. I'll give you some money."

"It ain't *giving* me money," she spat. "It's money you owe for staying here."

I took a breath, slapped my hands on my thighs, felt the sting of an aggressive smack and turned away. "I'll be down the hall if you need anything." I made a point not to tell her specifically that I was staying in Ori's room. My old room was also down the hall; she didn't need to know right now.

Michael left with me, followed me to Ori's bedroom door. "You want to hang out on the roof for old times' sake?" he asked.

The way nostalgia hit knocked the air out of me. Michael hadn't asked me to spend time with him since we were kids and he'd ask me to play hide-and-seek. It felt good, like part of our broken family might be trying to glue itself back together. "Sure."

We walked back down the hall to his bedroom and crawled out of his window where the roof for the downstairs bathroom was. It had been a long time since we'd both sat out under the stars together, but watching the rain move in would have to suffice.

He pulled out a joint and lit it, passed it to me. I took a drag, then another and handed it back.

"I heard you and your girl broke up."

I snapped my eyes to him. "Laurel just can't shut up, can she?"

He huffed a laugh and then found his normal aloof self. "You shouldn't talk shit about Mom. And you should call her Mom."

"What the fuck?" I took a drag, handed it back to him and laid back, letting my eyes drift as far upward as they could.

"I should be asking you about Dahlia. How are you?" I slapped at a mosquito on my leg.

"I don't want to talk about it."

"I understand." I pinched my fingers at him so he'd pass the joint back.

"She's gone," he said, turning his head away from me to blow out of stream of smoke. "Talking about her won't bring her back." His energy sank, and I felt him drift from me emotionally.

I stared out into the darkness, frogs chirping along the swamp banks, fireflies flashing their bellies to assure me the darkness wasn't growing closer...shame they were wasting their pretty glow on this place.

The quiet lasted a long while, both of us laid on our backs, our eyes to the sky. I wondered what life might have been like if Laurel hadn't married a pedophile. We might have moved into her mother's house in South Carolina where my grandma would have kept a watchful eye out for us kids. She was the protector, and once she died Laurel abandoned me.

"Johnna?" Michael's voice cracked.

I turned to him. "Yeah?"

"I saw you that day." He sat up, so I did.

"What day?"

"I saw you twist Barrett's breathing tube closed. I watched you kill him."

My ears hummed, static rolling across my skin, panic knocking at my captain's door. It wanted to be inside the cabin where it could hijack me completely. But I knew I couldn't deflect, spin a lie that he'd believe. I was tired of hiding my sin. "Why didn't you tell on me?"

"He was a piece of shit. He deserved to die for what he did to you."

My stomach dropped, and my heart filled with fondness and appreciation for my brother. All these years I thought no one in my family believed me, but he did. Maybe I could trust him now.

"I didn't tell you everything," I said, blowing out smoke and passing back to him.

He took a drag, his brows creased, and when he blew out the smoke he said, "Everything about what?"

I wished I'd not said anything, but I had to tell him. "I was the one who found her car." I watched him to see how he'd react.

He pulled the joint back up to his lips and sucked it halfway down. "How?" he said through plumes of smoke.

I looked up at the stars, sparse as they were since clouds covered most of the night sky. "It was in the Hager garage. Kimber found me there. He attacked me. Choked me out and put me in her car then drove it to the Cape and pushed it in, me strapped in the seatbelt." I couldn't bear to look at my brother. His breaths were choppy, like mine got when I was about to have a panic attack.

"Did you tell the police?" He stared, waiting for my response.

"Yes, I—"

He smacked the butt of his hand to his forehead. "Fucking Christ, Johnna." His feet shifted and he lost balance, stumbling to catch a footing. "Goddamnit," He stomped to the window and crawled through.

CHAPTER TWENTY

Ori's bed wasn't hospitable, not with memories of the swamp thing attacking me still fresh. I wasn't sure if I'd see the corpse ghost again...but it wouldn't be for lack of trying. I lay down, then went to Ori's social and scoured through her photos again, hoping, praying for a clue. I had a true crime podcast playing on my laptop, and soaked in everything I heard, as if listening to a few podcasts would give me a leg-up from the detectives working the case now. Ori's posts had begun to feel familiar; I'd scrolled through them a million times. Frustrated, I dropped the phone to my side and stared at the ceiling, counting all the glow-in-the-dark stars. I'd helped her put them there long ago.

I thought about the picture of her and Kimber, his face too close to hers for my comfort, and I wondered...what might he have on his social? I picked up my phone and googled Kimber Hager, and nothing, not even an old Facebook popped up. The only thing that came remotely close to Kimber being on the internet was an obituary about his father with him and his brothers named as the only remaining family.

Nothing made sense. I understood why he tried to kill me,

but what did Ori do? Or Dahlia for that matter. Why would Kimber murder Dahlia and his brother and likely Ori?

"Hmm...what about Jamie." Seems like a good place to search since he was just found dead in the trunk of her car. Jamie's social was easy to find, and surprisingly full of pictures. Pictures of fishing boats and photo-worthy catches. Pictures of the river and the garage, of the coffee place in town and the burger joint. He had a picture of nearly every business in Sweetwater, even one of him walking out of the police station with his hands behind his back in a fake hand-cuffed pose, Shannon laughing in the background. That picture was followed by three from Shannon's police academy graduation. I zoomed in, traced the line of his face, remembering the times I thought he was heaven. He still hadn't contacted me. I'd ruined his world. Things would never be the same.

Moments later, I was thumbing through my text threads looking for Shannon's name. My finger hovered over the call button, but something stopped me.

So, I pulled back and flipped to Jamie's page again. Scrolled and scrolled until Ori's face began showing up. My interest piqued, my body leaning so close to my phone I could smell the chemical scent of a too hot battery. A few pics of Ori was reasonable. Jamie was Michael's BFF and they were always together, so it made sense he'd cross paths often with Michael's sister, but I still had nothing. I dropped the phone on the bed next to me, rolled my head to look at her dresser. A jewelry box, a small collection of seashells, some perfume bottles, her Polaroid...shit!

I jumped up and ran to the dresser, snatching up the camera. I remembered a few years back the brand-new Polaroid picture revolution. It was shocking how many young people were buying those things, me included. What photographer would pass up on the fun of instant photo hard copies. Ori would have used the crap out of that thing. There had to be pictures around here somewhere.

I tore through her drawers, trying to respect her belongings and stifling my eagerness to find evidence was a battle. I scoured through everything, dressers, boxes, books...but nothing to show for it except a few dust bunnies in my hair. It didn't make sense. Why would she have a Polaroid if she wasn't going to use it? I wanted to give up, to forget all of it, go home and get in my own bed, sleep until the new year.

I turned away from the dresser, eyed the underside of her bed, and found myself wiggling around in floor dust and old fallen popcorn. My phone light shot up into the box spring and it occurred to me then that if Ori had pictures to hide, they'd be somewhere a little less conspicuous.

I scooted out from under the bed and pored through my memory of true crime shows I'd watched. I recalled an episode from Columbine where one of the shooters taped their drawings to the back of their dresser. It was a great hiding place.

With all my strength I heaved the corner of the long, heavy dresser and managed to pull it a few inches from the wall. I nearly dropped my phone behind it while shining the light down. A sharp pain speared my brain when I saw nothing. I checked the second dresser, smaller, lighter, and still nothing.

"Fuck!" I threw my phone, regretting it instantly. It cartwheeled across the room and hit the dresser mirror, cracking it down the center.

Laurel was going to be pissed. "Shit." I crossed the room and picked up my phone then went to the broken mirror. I traced my finger down the crack, a knot growing in my chest. I thought about all the times she'd looked in that mirror, brushed her hair, tried on outfits, wiped off makeup. It would never reflect her image the same again because of me.

A sharp pain tore across my fingertip, and I jerked my hand

to my face, examining the sliced flesh. On instinct, I put my finger in my mouth and licked off the blood, looking back at the mirror to see a red drop streaking downward. Before I could catch it, my blood dripped onto the white doily underneath her jewelry box.

"Damnit." I hurried to clean it up, lifting her jewelry box and taking up the lace, rushing it to the bathroom sink, praying I could remove the blood with cold water before a stain set in. I'd already wrecked her mirror, ruining her doily would send me over the edge. I could barely keep my shit together without having this guilt hanging over me.

The water finally ran clear, the cut on my finger an afterthought; it didn't even hurt anymore. I hung the doily over the shower rod and went back to the dresser with a wad of toilet paper to clean up the mess. There was a bit of blood on the jewelry box leg, so I leaned it on its side to wipe it away, and that's when I saw the envelope taped to the bottom, JAMIE written in purple marker.

"Holy shit." I pushed my finger into the opening and flipped it open, and my heart jumped when I saw the Polaroids. I snatched them out, flipped them over to see what selfies looked like in the 80s. Ori, her long black hair and big eyes pursing duck lips; Ori taking a hit from a joint, and then...Ori kissing Jamie. I shook my head, as if I could shake away the images. Another and another of the two making out, posing, half naked in some. On one of the pictures, a date was written: Feb 14th, 2022. Another one, more graphic, hands underneath clothes taken a week later. More and more, some more cringe than others. My stomach shriveled, sour climbing my throat.

She was with Gabe then, had been for a year, he'd mentioned, so why the hell was Ori kissing *Jamie*?

I heard Jamie's voice in my mind, screaming how Ori was a

whore. She might have been playing two guys, but she didn't deserve to be killed.

"Mother fucker." Jamie was with Ori. Maybe Kimber was jealous? I needed to tell Michael what I'd found.

My feet hit the hardwoods with a thump, and I stomped all the way to Michael's bedroom. "Hey." I knocked on his door as quietly as I could—Laurel was still sleeping. Though, she was so dosed on cold meds it'd take a bottle whack to the head to wake her.

"Michael!" I reached for the knob; it was locked. "Goddamnit." I forgot he said he wanted to go work on his truck in the barn, and I didn't feel like walking all the way out there. I dialed his number, heard his phone ringing on the other side of the door. He must have smoked one of those special joints he warned me away from.

I leaned against the door, my phone pressed against my chin while my mind puzzled over a hundred scenarios.

My mind was a beehive hit with a rogue ball from a child playing too close, all chaos and buzzing. This town was too small for an affair among friends and while my mind tried to make excuses for Shannon, my heart knew that he knew about it, but had said absolutely dick to me.

***

Water spilled over the glass and cold dripped down my hand. My train of thought was on Gabe and not the kitchen tap. I turned it off, pulled the glass to my lips and drank the water down. Still thirsty, I refilled and gulped down a second glass. Then I raided the fridge, pulled out some KFC, sniffed it, and plopped it on the table and searched the condiments shelf for hot sauce before closing the fridge. Laurel put everything in the fridge, even peanut butter, which sucked because cold peanut butter is nasty.

I didn't bother reheating the chicken strips, just doused them in hot sauce and chomped down. I must have gone through half the bottle before I was done, and still I wanted to turn it up and chug it. I stopped as the little spicy spout touched my lips. "What the hell, Johnna?" I pulled the bottle away and sat it on the table.

Michael's weed must have been a different batch than the one I'd had in his truck because I didn't even think of food after I'd smoked that one. Anyway, I'd made myself at home and ate all the leftovers and figured I should replenish them first thing tomorrow in case Laurel was well enough to come downstairs for food. She'd be pissed if there was nothing to eat.

"Ha." I laughed a little too loud, heard my voice travel through the entire house like a thief that had just knocked over a glass vase on marble flooring. Fucking crypt.

I walked into the living room and turned on the television, not planning on watching anything; I just wanted noise, but Shanique was covering the discovery of Ori's car, so I sat.

"Police still haven't released the identity of the body found inside the missing woman's trunk, but investigators say they will have more information by morning. Channel Four news, I'm Shanique Rollins."

The news cut to commercial, a family sitting at a dinner table, typical shit you'd expect on evening television. Nothing like what my family looked like, or a lot of the families I knew. It was a hard life in these parts, but Rhel's family always sat for dinner together. I stayed with her so often that her mom would set me a place at the table even if I wasn't there through force of habit.

CHAPTER TWENTY-ONE

Morning sun warmed my face, the night had been cool from the weather front that dumped buckets of rain on the area, and I had slept with the windows open. I laid there, in Ori's bed, on her pillow, watching the curtains blow, letting the breeze dance its fingers across my arms, its soft caress throwing me to a memory of the day I killed Barrett. I had watched him for so long, standing in the doorway, praying for each breath to be his last. But it never was. Until I intervened.

I rolled over, stretched my body, the tension flowing out like pus from a lodged splinter that'd been under too long. I was off, the dream eating away at me.

I knew I'd find the whole truth, but first I had to call Shannon. I felt around the covers for my cell, and when I didn't find it, I slapped the nightstand, looking over when my fingers hit the phone, dried mud crusted over them. I jolted up.

"What the fuck!"

I turned my hands over, the mess dried down to my elbows. "Oh my God." I flew to the bathroom, and looked in the mirror, dirt smeared across my face. What the hell had happened? My heart pounded, heat flushing my face.

I jumped, ran to get Michael and didn't bother knocking. I twisted the knob; the door opened, and I bolted inside.

"Michael?" I called out to an empty room. Maybe he was downstairs. I ran to the banister, then stopped in my tracks. I didn't know if Laurel would be down there too, and she'd have a lot of questions. I was covered in dirt when even I didn't know why. I stood there, steadying my thoughts to plan my next move, my eyes falling past the banister spindles, landing on the muddy footprints leading from the front door, up the stairs, and—I craned my neck around the railing post—into Ori's room. "Oh shit," I whispered.

I ran back to her room, scanned the floor, barefoot mud tracks going straight to the bed. "No no no no no." My breath stopped in my throat, fear strangling me. I stared down at the footprints, walked slowly toward them and placed my foot inside. A perfect fit.

Everything inside me locked up. I wanted to scream, to run, to explode. Instead, I stared, let my mind cycle through a million horrible possibilities until the scariest one flashed in my mind. Had I been sleepwalking again? I hadn't taken Ambien since the night I walked my sleeping ass straight down a flight of stairs. I rushed to the bathroom, my feet matched every step, filling them perfectly, making me sicker. What was going on? The question stirred in my mind, a dizzying tornado of anxiety. I thrust my arms under the tap, hissed at the pain on my fingertips when water hit them, and scrubbed like the mud was acid, burning through to the bone. The water swirled in a dark brown and red pool, my fingertips in flaming pain. I pulled them up close: fingernails and meat missing in small chunks across all my fingers. I wiped dry, spot checked, changed my clothes and ran downstairs, checking over my body with each step.

A knock.

I froze, the silent house telling me Laurel wasn't in the

living room watching TV and by line of sight she and Michael weren't in the kitchen. I opened the door, found Shannon standing on the other side, not in uniform.

I almost choked on my tongue. "Hi," I said, keeping the door closed as much as possible. I wasn't sure what he knew about Jamie. "Your boss was looking for you."

He nodded. "I've talked to him."

My skin flushed hot, still unsure if I could trust him. "Where have you been? I was worried about you."

He fidgeted, uncomfortable in his own skin. "I just needed to blow off some steam. Then I found out about Jamie and..."

I wanted to trust him in that moment, his soul bared, heartbroken. "I'm so sorry, Shannon."

"I need to talk to Michael." And just like that, he was a stranger in front of me, tone dead flat, unfamiliar.

His callousness took me off guard. "Um, I don't think he's here."

"You sure?" He leaned forward, some attempt to catch a better look inside I guessed. As if I were lying.

"I'm sure," I said, stepping out onto the porch, the doorknob in my hand as I held the door cracked behind me. "Shannon, what's going on?" He turned to leave, and I reached out, grabbing his arm. "Shannon? Why do you need to see Michael?"

He turned back around, eyes tracking behind me. I'd forgotten about the heavy door and how it always swung open. He saw the mess. "What's all that?"

I turned, gestured to the muddy floor, "Oh that." I had to think fast. "I heard a cat or raccoon in the trash and ran out to shoo it away. I was pretty out of it and didn't notice I tracked up the whole house." I forced a smile.

He drew his eyes down the length of me. "You don't look muddy."

I shoved my hands behind my back. "And you don't look happy to see me." When he didn't shift attitude, I said, "I washed up already."

"Hm," he grumbled, aloof.

"Well, I need to clean this up before Laurel sees it and cusses me until the cows come home."

"Yeah, okay." He bolted down the steps, slammed his car door and peeled off, spitting mud everywhere.

I hadn't seen that side of him before and didn't like it one bit. Obviously, something was going on and Michael was involved, which is probably why he kept quiet. Who would want to tell their lover that the police were searching for her criminal brother and her missing, presumed dead sister? Not Shannon. But what had Michael done? Was he a suspect for Dahlia? Boyfriends usually were, and I sure as hell gave Gabe a hard time about it. Practically forced the police on him.

After standing on the porch a moment, I noticed Laurel's car was gone. If Michael had it, then where was Laurel? I went back inside, walked through to the laundry closet, and fetched a mop and bucket to clean up the mess.

———

The porch swing creaked as I pushed off the weather-beaten boards with my feet, toking on the last joint I had. I decided to call Michael.

"Hey."

"Hey. Where are you?"

"Camping at Wilford's Cliff for the weekend. You should come."

"I don't know. I need to tell Laurel about Ori's car and all that."

"I told her this morning."

"What the hell, Michael?"

"What? She needed to know."

He wasn't wrong. "How'd she take it?"

"Exactly how you would think she'd take it. Listen I gotta go." Click.

A car engine echoed down the driveway. I waited outside to see who it was, didn't recognize the white hatchback when it pulled up, but Laurel got out and the driver left with little more than a nod.

"Who was that?" I stood to open the door, Laurel's hands full of Dollar Tree bags and one very stocked black liquor store bag.

"What do you think? I ain't got no way to get around? They're called friends, Johnna." She walked inside without thanking me for holding the door.

"You have a car," I said, letting the screen door slap closed behind me as I followed her into the kitchen. I needed to see how she really was handling the news about Ori and besides, she'd been so ill yesterday. I couldn't trust that she wouldn't fall sick again any minute. I prayed not though; I didn't feel like Susie Homemaker right then.

"Michael needs my car for the weekend."

Yup he needs it to party all weekend. "You look better."

"No thanks to you. You just kept me dosed up on that nasty shit and left me alone."

Bitch, you're lucky I did that much. "I was here the whole time, Momma. I checked on you, cooled you down with a washcloth. Me and Michael both."

She ignored me, kept throwing groceries into cabinets, the worn doors smacking shut as she hurried without care, and I was surprised she'd gone this long without mentioning Ori's car. She had to be worried same as me. But I didn't want to upset her by bringing it up right now.

She pulled the last grocery item from the plastic bag, instant mashed potatoes, and flung them into the cabinet, slamming it shut. "Would it have killed you to buy some groceries while I was sick?" She wadded the plastic bags into a ball in her fists and leaned against the counter, eyes glaring.

My jaw dropped. "Momma, I—"

"Why are you so difficult?" Her eyes narrowed as they lingered, but after an awkward silence, she turned to another cabinet and opened the door, reaching in for a rocks glass.

Whatever sympathy I had for her died just then. I didn't; care if my questions upset her. I wanted to find my sister, and I could feel something awful was close enough to home to pry. "I know Michael told you about the police finding Ori's car."

Laurel leaned her body into the cabinet door she was holding, slammed it so hard it bounced and slapped shut a second time. "What is with you?" She turned angrily toward me, rested her palms flat on the kitchen table as she leaned closer. "You perpetuate death. I've seen those pictures you take to make all that money. You ain't right. Normal people don't occupy themselves with shit like that, but you? You just love it don't you? You'd love your sister to be dead. Maybe you could snap some prize-winning photos of her!"

I swallowed bile, settled the snarl twisting my mouth, and ran upstairs to pack an overnight bag.

I walked down the drive to meet the taxi and didn't say a word to Laurel when I left. She could rot in that fucking house for all I cared. "Take me to Wilford's Cliff," I confirmed with the driver; she nodded.

We'd been on the road a few minutes before I noticed the

driver's stolen glances in the rearview. She saw I'd caught her and said, "You're Ori Kern's sister, right?"

It wasn't her fault, asking. The shit was all over the news, and I hadn't prepared myself for that yet. I lifted my hand to prop on the door ledge, but when my eyes landed on my Band-Aid fingertips, I dropped it to my side. "Yep." I didn't glance back up, hoping she'd get the hint that I didn't want to talk about it, especially to a stranger.

"They found anything yet?"

Christ, guess she didn't get the hint. "You should watch the road."

"You don't have to be a bitch about it; the whole town's curious." She turned the radio on, turned it up loud and smirked.

We parted ways at my drop-off, neither of us giving courtesy to the other. Muffled noises of people yelling and playing music and the smell of early afternoon mosquito fires peeked through the trees. I made my way to the campsite, heard someone shout my name. I turned, saw Michael waving me over.

"You came!" He hugged me up, and I patted his back.

"I don't think we've ever hugged," I said, and he let me go.

"No time like the present." There had to be a pharmacy full of drugs in his system. I'd never seen him this carefree, happy. He was a whole other person. I preferred this Michael. Too bad the asshole part of him was never too far behind. I almost felt the urge to clock it...like how long would it take for one of these other drunks to piss him off, make him fly off the handle? For now though, I'd hang with him, see if I could find out why Shannon was looking for him.

"I'll have some of that." I snatched the joint he was holding; he laughed.

"Whoa, sis, that's the crazy shit." He reached for it, but I took a drag before he could snatch it. "Ah haha! You're crazy."

His laugh rolled off the water's surface, a nearby woman, young, pretty, extremely drunk, climbing for her turn on the rope swing. I'd jumped off that janky rope so many times. Childhood on a stick. The simplest, most fun thing to do at the riverbank was to swing off a rope.

I scanned the partygoers, wondering if any of them were involved with Ori's disappearance. There was no trust for me; everyone was a suspect until I knew otherwise. I thought about Dahlia and how these people must have known her too if they were hanging around Michael all the time. And that's when I figured out the reason for the awkward vibe. They were all scared.

I turned to Michael, watched him gaze at the crowd. Was he thinking about Dahlia? "Hey"—I nudged him playfully—"want to go for a swim?"

He shook his head, looked out across the river.

I took one more drag when he passed the joint, and by the time I exhaled, the noises of everyone had wormed into my mind, splashing and yelling, music blaring; they all squirmed in my ears like some awful maggot infestation of sound.

I stumbled toward the river.

"You shouldn't get in the water on this shit," Michael shouted.

Diluted from the drugs coursing through me, I didn't answer, my tongue glued to the roof of my mouth. Nothing in the world seemed to matter, not even Ori's disappearance, which now seemed more of a plot I'd read in a book and less like my own life. I reached the edge where brown waters lapped the muddy bank, algae burping as the waters rose and fell from all the commotion. I pointed my arms above my head, bounced off my feet and dove in, the world sinking above me.

Under the water, I let out just enough air to keep me

submerged. I didn't want to open my eyes: the burn from doing that when I woke up in Ori's car was a lesson learned.

Warm rushed over me. It could have been the drugs, the pressure of water surrounding me—I was numb. I didn't feel anything, not the temperature of the water or the aching in my soul. I was completely relaxed, unburdened...at peace. And just as I relaxed, something grabbed me.

My eyes flew open, and I saw.

Ori. Her face was hollow, like a doll with its eyes cut out. Her hair drifted like a cobweb on the water's surface. She wrapped her arms around me, clamping her hand over my mouth. I started sinking lower and lower beneath the murky waters. Air bubbles shot out of the spaces between her boney, cold fingers as I screamed.

I struggled, kicked, dug my nails into her arms as I wrenched them away, her bloated flesh curling under my nails. Her grip loosened and I kicked to the surface, gasping as I broke through the water.

CHAPTER TWENTY-TWO

I swam to the bank, palms slapping the slimy edge as I dug my fingers in and pulled myself out. I stayed there, on my hands and knees, and coughed in the fresh air. Above me, voices clashed, an exchange of deep, commanding tones. I looked up, saw Shannon and Michael face to face, veins popping out of Michael's neck like they always did when he was angry. Shannon pushed a finger into Michael's chest, jaws clenched, a pointed glare and Michael stepped forward, spitting words, baring teeth.

I climbed to my feet, slipped in the mud as I struggled to stand, and finally got a foothold. I walked quickly, carefully toward the tent, other campers running into me or in front of me as I scrambled to stay upright; bare feet and mud were a poor combination. "Hey!" I called, but they couldn't hear me and before I could get back to the tent, Shannon took off, the trees smuggling him away.

I reached the tent—Michael hadn't noticed me there yet—and called after Shannon, but he didn't reply. I glanced at Michael, who was looking at me by then, bottom jaw jutted out as he tried to keep the fire from barreling out of him. I pivoted to chase after Shannon, but Michael grabbed my arm, yanking me back. "You don't want to be around him right now; he's not thinking straight."

I snatched away my arm. "Don't tell me what I need." I took another step.

He grabbed me again. "Johnna, that joint was laced with ketamine. Do you really want to be around a cop right now?"

No, I really didn't. But I already knew Michael wouldn't tell me shit even if I asked. "Then what the hell was that?"

Michael tipped up his beer bottle, took a swig, "He's just an asshole, I guess. Didn't like finding out that I gave you a laced joint."

"You told him!" I got in his face. "Why did you do that Michael? What I do is my business."

The faintest grin teased his lips. "Well, he's a cop and I have a shit ton of drugs here. So I figured if he knew you were participating in my festivities, he'd leave me alone about it."

I hate my life. "You're an asshole." I stomped away, then stopped turning back to him. "Was he asking about Kimber?"

He glared across the river. "No."

Fuck fuck fuck. "Alright then. I'm going home. See ya later."

I tried to puzzle out where I left my car, then realized I'd taken a taxi. I pulled my phone from my pocket. Water dripped out of the casing. "Fuck!"

My hair stuck in tendrils to my neck and cheeks, and my wet denim shorts were already chafing between my legs. My ears played a *wa-wa* sound that pulsed in my skull like a soundtrack to a bad horror movie. *So, this is what a ketamine high feels like, huh?*

I hated it. And I hated myself for smoking Michael's joint knowing there was something in it that I hadn't put there myself. Sure, I'd crushed some Ativan in my weed before, but it was nothing like this. "Ugh." I grabbed my stomach, nausea sloshing back and forth inside me.

Out of the woods at a main dirt road, I flagged down a car, a group of girls giggling inside.

"What's up, chicken butt?" the driver asked, her face bright with fun. A girl in the backseat blew out a plume of vape that smelled like candy and despite my efforts not to react to it, the unease in my stomach rose up my throat and I gagged it back down. "Are y'all heading back to town?"

"Yep." She pointed to the girl vaping in the backseat. "This one is still underage so, we gotta get her home before her mom sends the dogs." She cast a coy glance back at the girl.

"So, my mom's a bitch." The girl shrugged and then disappeared into her phone, the screen illuminating her face, old eye makeup running from a hot and humid Carolina day.

"Can I catch a ride?" I grabbed my stomach, feeling some relief as it started to settle.

"Yeah. Hop in."

I walked around the front of the car, headlights casting my shadow in the trees. "Thanks," I said, closing the door.

The driver peeled out, throwing mud behind us, and she laughed like she'd just pulled off the world's most dangerous stunt. "Did y'all see that?" she boasted, one hand on the wheel, the other thumbing over her phone screen.

"You shouldn't text and drive." I was officially an old lady now.

"I'm not texting." She placed the phone down on the seat and a loud orchestra of sound blurred from the car speakers. I recognized the song, a band I discovered a few months prior. "Kavinsky?" I said, not quite sure I had the name right.

She nodded. "*Night Call.*"

Yeah... that was it. I loved the song. Played it on repeat at least a hundred times when I had first heard it. Danae was so tired of hearing it that she'd walk out of the room whenever I played it, eyes so far in the back of her head I wasn't sure they'd ever go to center again.

"You're that missing girl's sister, aren't you?"

I wiped my nose; river water was still finding its way back out of me. "Yep."

"Johnna?"

"Yes." I turned to her, eager to know if she knew anything. "Did you know Ori?"

She retreated, sunk into herself the way I had when Barrett came around, but no matter how hard I tried to be invisible, it never worked. I didn't like that she felt that way now, even if she might have known Ori, so I let out a laugh. "It's okay if you're afraid to talk. I know how hard it is living in a small town. Nothing ever stays a secret." As soon as those words left my mouth I wanted to scream. I wondered how many people in town knew about Barrett...the things he'd done to me? Had Shannon told anyone all those years ago when I leaned on him? Did Laurel spill her view of me as a liar to her friends while she was drunk?

She smiled, sat up a bit straighter. "I hope they find her."

Her reply was sincere. "Thank you." I reached for the heater knob, suddenly cold and momentarily oblivious that I wasn't in my own car, but before my finger hit the button... "Can I? Just for a second."

"Sure boo. Nothing like a ketamine high to make you flush from hot to cold so quickly." She smudged an in-the-know smile on her lips.

I didn't like that she knew I was on drugs. That was a private thing I did with Michael, and I hadn't really wanted anyone to know except for us. I'd heard enough shit talked about Laurel when she was busy making her name around town, the kind of name you didn't want to be associated with. So as an adult, I'd made it my business to keep a private image of my person. The outside world didn't need an inside look at Johnna LaGrange; the outside world didn't deserve it. I picked up a wet strand of my hair. "I'm just cold from the river."

"Whatever you say, girl." Her eyes flashed to the rearview, the girl in the backseat trading grins. I wanted to stretch the lie, make them believe me somehow, but they were right, and they knew it...must have had enough experiences of their own, which only made it harder to convince them I was just cold. I reached for the heater, turned it off, then cursed under my breath that I was so fucking hot.

CHAPTER TWENTY-THREE

When I woke up in Ori's bed, my heart immediately swelled, and anxiety slithered over me like so many snakes. My eyes flicked down to my hands, clean...the bedsheets, clean...and no sign of anything on the floor. I scrambled for my phone, cringed when I felt the smooth wood of a vacant nightstand and remembered taking it on my river adventure.

I went downstairs to the kitchen phone and called Shannon. No answer.

I called again.

Voicemail.

"Shit." I called Michael. No answer. That wasn't too concerning since it was only—I looked at the kitchen clock— nine in the morning. All the river rats were still in drug-induced comas.

I wasn't at all surprised to see Laurel still slumped over on the couch in the same position she was when I got home last night. Only now, the vodka bottle had fallen from her hand and onto the floor. The TV was still turned down; I had to lower the volume last night when I got in because it was so loud, I could hear it in Ori's room with the door shut. "See ya later, Momma," I said, voice too low for her to hear, even if she were awake. And I didn't bother to catch the screen door as I ran out.

It'd take me thirty minutes to walk to town. Sweat ran down my back, heat like it was mid-July, and the cloud coverage was the only thing keeping me from not 100 per cent regretting that I'd walked.

A shortcut through the woods put me out between two old brick buildings on Main Street. One was a consignment store, a marquee sign on the sidewalk telling us that everything is thirty per cent off. I'd have gone in normally, but today was not that day. Too far gone were days anywhere close to normal.

The other building was a barbershop, the old-fashioned barber's pole stagnant, broken since I could remember. I stepped onto the sidewalk, hardly took another step before the clash of media and police vehicles blocking off the road ahead stopped me dead.

I ducked back behind the barber shop. I didn't want attention, and certainly not to be caught while a reporter was live on air. I poked my head back around, old brick scratching my fingertips as I gripped the corner. I circled behind the consignment store and crossed the street, walking up a parallel back street and into the gas station, flinching when the door squeaked and two patrons turned to gawk at me.

I ducked into an aisle, baby diapers and pain reliever, automotive oils...nothing I needed. I headed straight to the coolers in the back, opened the door and pulled out a bottle of water, opening the cap and drinking before I'd paid. I must have gulped it half down before stopping, checking to see that the clerk had been watching me, a woman too young to look as old as she did.

I wondered if she was staring because I was sampling the merchandise or because she recognized me. I tried to recall her, filtered through as many high-school faces as I could remember to see if any were hers. After coming up with nothing, I assumed she'd stop staring if I moved up to the check-out.

Last in line, I plopped the empty bottle on the counter along with a full one. "And a pack of Camel Lights." I hated cigarettes, but I was out of pot and pills, and if I didn't get something in me to calm my ass down, I was going to vibrate into oblivion, or hit up a liquor store.

The attendant dipped below the counter and stood back up with the cigs. "Horrible what's happening, ain't it?" Her eyes went outside to the incident.

"What happened?" I pulled out a twenty-dollar bill, wincing as I remembered that I'd ruined my phone, and handed it to her.

"They identified the body they found." Her tone closely flirting with fear.

My heart stopped beating. Hearing a random store clerk talk about what happened at the river made it more real and horrifyingly awful. "Who?" Small talk poured out in small towns. I knew it was Ori. Of course, I knew. And still.

"Kimber Hager." She looked down at my items. "Want a bag?"

I nearly choked, and though I tried to tell her I didn't want a bag, nothing came out. I snatched up my things and hurried for the door, pushed through them, the cigarette pack already ripped open and my fingernails pinching for the filter end. I bit my lips around it, struck a match from the pack I'd lifted off Laurel's living room table, and took a long drag, blowing the smoke into the sky. It felt nice at first, that whoosh of nicotine binding to my neurotransmitters, diffusing the chaos in my mind. And then the nausea hit, like the twin sister of *hungover* crashing the party.

But before I could duck into the back alley, a reporter spotted me. They came running, a stampede of eager faces, phones and mics outstretched. I turned to run, taking the nearest edge of the gas station, but I ended up at a fenced-in dumpster area and was blocked. The mass enveloped me, the clicks and pops of media equipment readying for the big show; it was like some kind of tabloid insect, all a part of one. My stomach flipped.

"Miss LaGrange, can you tell us..." so many voices shouted. They all sounded the same, uncaring, eager.

I tried to catch my breath, but the smell of perfume and armpits hit me. My vision was spinning, skin flashing hot to cold, a panic attack boiling to get out. I dropped my head, eyes forced to the pavement, a variety of shoes skipping this way and that, a particularly nice pair of stilettos that I recognized. Shanique? I didn't look up.

Instead, I pivoted, trying to avoid vomiting on her heels, but the urge was too strong and my conviction was weak. I buckled, vomit purging from me like the end of a water hose once the kink was suddenly straightened.

Everyone jumped back, a voice in the background shouting for everyone to disperse. Through it all, I managed to not get anyone, which would have been only slightly less embarrassing than puking in front of a dozen cameras.

"I said move!" Shannon ordered, and relief of him being there overrode the doubts I was having about him. I stood up straight, locked in on him bulldozing toward me, and when his arm went around me, I wanted to collapse into him. "I got you," he said, stiff-arming reporters to clear a path.

We darted through the crowd, pushed our way out and made it to his squad truck. The door closed and the noise of hustling life outside muffled just enough to breathe. But the longer we sat, the thicker the air grew, and I knew what was going through his mind.

"I heard. I'm sorry," was all I could manage. What else was I supposed to say? Sorry about the Hager brothers' bad luck? It took every morsel of self-control to keep my shit together. The unknown was burning a giant black hole in my chest. I had no idea how to sort any of this mess, and the longer I stayed the worse things got. I wanted to go home, but that option had left the moment I passed the old Sweetwater town sign, and I knew it then as well as I knew it now.

Shannon drove us to a secluded area near the marsh, where I watched the tree moss blow in the wind. I thought about the visions I'd had, Barrett, Ori, the claustrophobic swamps. My eyes blurred. I wiped them...looked over at Shannon, a locked expression, clenched jaw. "Shannon, I—"

"He was crushed to death by a commercial truck at the garage."

Marbles of guilt bulged in my throat. Guilt for thinking Shannon had killed Kimber. Guilt from knowing I was about to ask, *Did you have anything to do with it?* Laurel was right, I must like to stir shit up.

"I would do anything for you, Johnna, but I didn't kill my brother."

I believed him, but someone killed Kimber, and if it wasn't Shannon then who? And with Kimber dead, I wondered if it were someone else who killed Jamie now. "They were into bad things, Shannon. You know that. This is probably a retaliation of some sort." Which might mean that Dahlia and Ori could have been in the wrong place at the wrong time, saw something they shouldn't have.

He nodded, chewed on the inside of his bottom lip. "Is Michael home?"

Strange transition, but okay. "Why? What would Michael have to do with any of this?"

"Nothing, I just want to tell him myself about Kimber. I know they hung out a lot."

I wouldn't say Michael and Kimber were BFFs by any means, but Shannon was in despair, and I wasn't going to keep him from trying to function on what little bit of spirit he had left. "He's still at the river."

Shannon gripped the wheel, squeezed it then let go and threw his hands up. "I have to bring him in for questioning."

My face got hot. "What?"

"He's a suspect, Johnna. We can't just ignore—"

"That he's now a *Gabe* in all this?" I knew it was all procedure, but that procedure was the same a week ago and they never questioned Michael about Dahlia. Not formally. I was caught between pissed and afraid. "Shannon, Michael didn't kill anyone."

He laughed, forceful, uncontrolled. "You know better than most what people are capable of."

"Damn, Shannon. You really went there, didn't you?" He wasn't wrong but throwing it in my face that I was molested was harsh as fuck.

He took in a sharp breath. "You're right. I'm sorry, but—"

"But? Sure sounds like you're sorry to me." Now I was pissed. "What is it that you think he did here, Shannon? You think he killed our sister, and then decided to take down the biggest assholes in the county who—not to mention—are brothers to a cop? Cool cool cool." I tucked my hands between my legs, suddenly chilled. "I want to go home."

Air came out of him in a low hum. "I don't..." he sighed. "I just—"

"You just told me that I'm incapable of knowing my own brother because of what Barrett did."

"Johnna," his tone softened.

"Shannon." I stared at him, blinking. "Home, please."

CHAPTER TWENTY-FOUR

S hannon placed a kiss on my cheek and that was it. I got out
of his car and didn't watch him leave, though the sound of
his engine was louder than normal as I waited inside the front
door for his presence to be gone. Even still, his lips burned on
my flesh in a way that was both exciting and sad.

"I'm home," I called out, not wanting to scare Laurel if she
hadn't heard me arrive. I poked through the kitchen, checked
the living room, headed upstairs when I didn't find her.
"Momma?" I was at her door, knuckles on the wood ready to
knock. When she didn't answer, I pushed open the door,
stepped inside. Her bed was made, nothing unusual, so I walked
across the room to check her bathroom. "Momma? You in
there?" I knocked, then twisted the knob open when she didn't
reply.

Vacant.

After searching upstairs, I crept back downstairs, looking for
a note on the kitchen table or refrigerator, assuming she might
have left a clue for Michael as to her whereabouts.

Nothing.

I noticed the back door cracked open, stepped through it

outside and looked toward the barn. Maybe she'd gone to check on Michael's progress at fixing his truck. The path was still soggy from all the rain, mud squishing into the soles of my shoes. My steps were unsteady in the muck, I slipped several times, dropping to a knee once. When I hit the ground, a vision jolted behind my eyes. I saw myself, rather felt myself in a memory, a memory of me digging in the dirt. My fingertips were bloody, rock and root having ripped away my flesh. Yet I dug, still. Faster, more eager, like a mindless robot. Only, I had no idea what I was digging for. Then it was gone, quickly as it came.

I stood. There was no point in trying to wipe off the mud, not since I had to walk all the way back too, and I was clumsy. But now I knew where the mud came from. My meds finally had me. I was sleepwalking again.

"Momma?" I yelled, hoping that if she were out there, I wouldn't have to walk all the way. I swatted at the gnats that kept flying at me, a stranger in their wood. I rounded the path, eyed the decrepit chicken coop, remembered a speckled hen we had when I was a kid. I'd picked it out at the farm store, and it was the first chicken that Laurel cooked when times fell hard.

I swear I heard a cluck, but kept moving, the path bleeding into the barn, a Gambrel with one long center bay, Laurel standing in the center, staring up at the bracer. I stared up, envisioned her hanging. My whole body flinched at the hallucination.

"Momma, what are you doing out here?"

Laurel didn't move, she only kept staring up.

I walked to her, slowly, my fingers reaching for the bend in her arm. "Momma," I whispered.

Her eyes turned down to me. "Ori?" she mumbled, face pale, sweat glinting off her clammy skin.

"No, Momma. It's Johnna." I reached out for her. "Come on, let me take you back to the house."

She didn't move when I gently tugged her toward me. "Momma?"

She kept staring up at the rafter. I stepped in front of her, took her face in my hands and tilted her chin down so I could see her eyes, glassed in alcohol, fully unaware.

"My baby," she croaked, then raised a knife I hadn't seen in her hand and jammed it into her neck.

"Mom!" I gasped, flinching in horror. "Oh my God!" Hands trembling, I reached for the knife. All the impulses needed to close my fingers around the handle fired properly but weren't fast enough to catch her before she buckled to the straw floor, a plume of barn dust rolling into the air.

"Shit!" I knelt, scooped her head in my hand and put pressure around the blade still lodged in her neck. "Momma. What did you do?"

Her eyes peeled open still, her breath smelling of rot, and the wound wouldn't stop pumping blood. I looked around the barn, not knowing exactly what I wanted to find, but then I saw Michael's work jumpsuit. I jumped up, yanked it from the stall door he'd flopped it over and wrapped it around her neck. "I'll be right back."

I ran back to the house, snatched the landline, and dialed 9-1-1.

I wasn't sure how long it took the ambulance to arrive...a century, five minutes. They felt the same.

"How long has she been like this?" a medic asked, as she rushed to Laurel's side.

"I don't know. I found her out here staring up at the rafters and then she…" I motioned to her neck. "That's when I called."

"Mrs. Kern, can you hear me?" The medic asked, and I noted the instant she saw Laurel's eyes, a drunk gone off the deep end.

"Has she taken any drugs?" They didn't look at me, their focus still assessing Laurel.

"Uh, I mean it's possible, but I don't think so. She'd been sick for a few days on and off, but then I thought she was getting better. She went to—"

"She's coding!" the medic yelled. Another EMT rushed over with a red box, dropped to his knees, pulled down Laurel's shirt and stuck two pads to her chest. "Clear!"

The other medic responded. "All clear!"

The box made a noise and Laurel's body buckled upward in an arch.

"We've got a heartbeat!"

The two EMTs got Laurel into the ambulance, and when the doors shut with me inside, I felt an end coming, something irreversible waiting for me.

I'd counted the blue patches on the tile, the beige ones…the black streaks of shoe scuff marks. I hit up the vending machine three times, walked two full laps around the hospital and tried calling Michael a million times from the nurses' station, and still no word about Laurel.

"Hey."

I looked up from the nail I'd been picking at to see Shannon, no uniform, tired eyes. "Hey," I said back, exhaust threading my tone.

"Any word yet?" He sat down next to me, put a hand on my knee.

"Guess you heard through the grapevine?"

He nodded.

"Nothing yet."

His hand left my leg, went up to my face and pushed a strand of my hair behind my ear. "I need to tell you something."

When I faced him, he dropped his hand away, turned his eyes to the windows where the setting sun was pulling down the night. "What is it?" I asked.

He cleared his throat. "I'm not supposed to be telling you this, but—"

"Hi, folks," the doctor said, startling me.

I stood; Shannon followed. "How is she?" I asked, squeezing my shaking hands.

The doctor, face lined with years of stress, shrugged. "She's still unconscious. We can't find anything, aside from the self-inflicted wound. Her blood tests came back normal...negative results for all common viral and bacterial tests. The EKG showed no signs of heart issues..." he shifted his glasses up his nose.

"What about brain function?" I knew to ask because of what happened with Danae.

"We did an MRI with dye, but it only showed some signs of reactive gliosis."

"What's that?"

"Typical in most people who suffer from migraines or have experienced some kind of central nervous system trauma...but these are non-threatening and would have nothing to do with what's happening to her now."

"So, what now then?" I tried not to sound like an ass, but it came off that way anyhow.

"She'll stay here until her injuries heal and then she'll go to a facility for a while."

"You mean a mental institution?"

"That's exactly right," he said, very plainly.

I wasn't leaving her. She didn't deserve my loyalty, but I wanted to stay. I turned to Shannon. "Can you get Michael? He should be here."

"Yeah, no problem. Do you need anything from the farmhouse?"

I shook my head, instinctively reached for my phone in my back pocket, felt my soul crush when my fingers didn't slide over the smooth Velvet Caviar case Danae bought for me, newspaper writing with a capital VC standing out. "Can you get me a prepaid phone?" I dug in my purse for my wallet, pulled my debit card and handed it out to him. "Here. My code is—"

"No. I'll take care of it. See you soon." He walked away, eyes scanning everyone as if suspects were abound. And maybe they were. It wasn't unusual for the criminal to be in places where they could witness their crime's effects.

I was alone with the doctor then. "Can I see her?"

"Of course." He turned, motioned me to follow. The hospital hallways loomed in dim lighting; a silence that could only be compared to a funeral home made the ringing in my ears louder, more defined. The smell was reminiscent of a childhood memory I couldn't quite place. I knew it had something to do with Laurel's side of the family, because she cried a lot.

"In there." The doctor pointed to a closed door.

"Thanks," I said softly, wishing he would have come in with me so I wouldn't be alone with her. I sat in the corner chair, didn't slide it closer to her bed the way I'd done when Danae was in ICU after her attempt. I wanted to climb in the bed with her that night, but I was afraid my angry pounding heart would disturb her. She didn't know I was even there.

I sat down, maneuvered on the faux leather awkwardly, the idea of it sticking to my skin another irk to add to the list of irks Laurel had brought into my life. I traced the contraptions around her bed with my eyes, the lead in her elbow bend, the patches on her upper chest, monitors detailing lines of information I only vaguely understood. Her face was pale, like the gray color of a skinned rabbit. I kept thinking about how I'd found her, just staring up like that, as if she'd been hypnotized by a bright light in the sky like in those alien abduction movies.

I hadn't expected to feel so uncomfortable alone with her. I'd been alone with her before, only recently when I was caring for her while she was sick. But something was different this time. She wasn't exactly herself in look or in vibe. I knew how to conduct myself around her, learned it as a child and evolved it as I grew, but sitting there then was as if I was with a total stranger who might be very unhappy with an unwanted observer. Laurel likely wouldn't want me there; she'd prefer Michael. But he wasn't there, and I was, and I was angry at him for that.

An hour had passed, and nothing changed in her. Shannon wasn't back and I wondered if he'd gotten called into work, unable to reach out to me. I walked out of the room and found the nurse's station. "Has anyone called for me?" I asked.

A young girl with a sharp nose and a pleasant smile set down a stack of papers. "What's your name?"

"Johnna LaGrange."

She clicked at the desktop. "Mmmm, nope. I'm not seeing anything." Her eyes flicked up to mine, a youthful spark too strong to hide behind her sympathy beamed back at me.

"Can I use the phone"—I looked down at her name tag— "Carley?"

"Sure." She left me, the sound of her mobile computer wheeling down the hall.

I dialed Shannon's number. He didn't answer. Then Michael's. No answer. I slammed down the phone. "Where the fuck are they?"

I turned and leaned against the desk, my eyes drifting down the long halls, still shots of the swamps and marshes, and other local scenery hanging on the walls. I imagined how the halls would look adorned with my photos, how inappropriate yet ironically accurate they'd be. Dead things, dying things, wounded things, that's all this place was.

Foot beats came rushing up from behind. "Hurry!" A nurse shouted, calm and firm. Shocked by the commotion, I watched as a team ran into Laurel's room.

"Shit!" I ran, stopping in the doorway as my eyes took in the scene of blood, so much blood.

My world was in slow motion, voices of the nurses around me muffled, distant, bogged down by my inability to process what I saw.

"You can't be in here!" A nurse tried to lead me out of the room.

I didn't budge. Not because I was trying to be difficult; I just couldn't move.

"What happened in here?" Carley asked, accusatory daggers in her eyes.

I saw Laurel then, slumped on the floor, blood from her wrists pooling in Carly's hands. A trail led from Laurel's body along the floor and to the wall where my eyes followed until I saw the drawings, finger painted from her own blood. A barn, and another, three then four and finally a fifth one. The paintings were scribbled across the whiteboard, the television, the window, and back down to the floor where she lay. "I don't know. I was out there on the phone."

"And you didn't hear anything?"

Laurel moaned. "Barn."

I looked at the pictures again, then my heart stopped, breath caught in my throat. It was the barn at the farmhouse.

"Ma'am, you need to leave," the same nurse persisted.

I pushed past her, finally having control of myself, and ran over to Laurel, dropping to my knees beside her. "What's at the barn, Momma?" Her body thrashed, arms flailing, Carley struggling to grab them out of the air and hold them in place.

Another nurse rushed over, snatched an arm, and began wrapping the six-inch vertical gash along Laurel's wrist. Laurel's body went stiff, her eyes rolling, mouth pulled down so tight veins in her neck were bulging.

"Momma, what's at the barn?" I shouted.

A nurse pushed me away and I fell backward onto my hands. "She's going to die if you don't get out of our way," Carley said, factually.

"Momma!" I shouted again.

Laurel's body jolted to life, and she threw herself at me, the nurse's grips loosened by surprise. She landed right in front of my face, her body over me, her hands planting on either side of me as I struggled to hold myself steady on my palms. Her eyes, white orbs lined in black, glared into me, through me.

"Momma?" I whimpered. "What's at the barn."

She moved inches closer, her face bending, contorting, breaking.

I froze. Everything inside me that made me exist stopped, and when the bones and skin on her face stopped moving, Ori's face staring back at me, she leaned into my ear, a chorus of cracking and clicking bubbled up her throat. And then she whispered. "Me."

CHAPTER TWENTY-FIVE

Laurel went limp on top of me, and I collapsed, the back of my head smacking the cold, hard floor. Two nurses were on her in a heartbeat, lifted her off and immediately tended to her wounds. "Are you okay?" A third nurse asked me, her eyes unblinking, frightened at what we'd all just seen. She helped me sit up, checked the back of my head before I knew she was even looking.

"I'm fine," I said in a whimper, touching the place I'd hit. When my hand came back dry, I was more confident in my own response.

"You sure?" She stood, held out a hand to help me up.

I grabbed her hand and pulled myself up. "Yeah." I stole another glance at Laurel, who had been lifted on the bed by then, the third nurse joining the effort to stop Laurel's bleeding. "Did any of you see that?"

"We all saw it, Miss LaGrange." The nurse replied, still busying herself with Laurel.

But I wasn't convinced she knew what I was talking about. "No...did you see her face when she jumped on me?"

"It looked like the face a very ill patient."

No one saw, which means what I saw wasn't real. I backed out of the room, still shocked, and bumped into another person rushing in to assist.

Outside the room, Laurel's door now shut, was like nothing at all was happening inside, an indistinguishable voice here and there, but that could be confused with casual conversation had I not known what was happening inside. I turned, a dizzying path of hallways before me. I shook my head, rubbed my eyes to clear the haze, and was able to tell which hall would lead me to the phone.

I ran down the hall, brown patient doors whizzing by in a blur. I ran until the counter at the nurses' station stopped me, my torso flopping over it as I reached across for the phone. Thankfully, the station was abandoned—the nurses were all in Laurel's room trying to keep her alive.

"Hi." I was trying to control my breath, but the fear still sat on my skin like oil. "I need a cab at the hospital."

Waiting for the elevator stirred my panic, so I rushed to the stairs, slung open the doors and ran down to the lobby as fast as I could. A young security guard in an oversized hospital-issued uniform looked up from their phone. "Ma'am, slow down please."

I ignored him as I tore through the double doors leading outside.

When the cab pulled up, I jumped inside. "Take me to 1712 Back Road."

He turned around, gray hair down to his shoulders, old baseball hat fraying on the bill. "Sweetwater?"

"Yeah." I nodded.

At the farmhouse, I threw open the car door, some sort of gibberish flying out of my mouth in the form of thanking the driver. I didn't wait for him to leave before running toward the barn, my heart in my throat, mind spinning. Laurel looked like Ori when she jumped on top of me...said she was at the barn. I wasn't sure exactly what that meant, but my gut kept yelling the answer, a sea of nausea thrashing the shores of my resolve. And when I remembered the memory of me digging near the barn, I ran to the sink and puked.

Nighttime was thick at the farmhouse...no streetlights, a cloudy sky snuffing the moon and stars, but I knew the path to the barn pretty well, despite the fact that it was overgrown now since Michael had been left in charge of the grounds. Laurel hadn't mentioned it, but I'd noticed the mowing tractor wasn't around. I assumed Michael sold it to maintain his party lifestyle.

Tall grass nipped my shins, little slashing stings as I ran through their sharp blades, but one must have been a rogue rose vine, and when it hit my leg it latched on, sinking deep. The pain shocked my nerves, and I fell, the damn thing still lodged in my skin by so many thorns. In the dark, I couldn't see well enough to extract the vine with a precision that meant less pain, so I just grabbed it and ripped. "Ungh," I winced, gritting my teeth until my jaw popped. But it was out now, and the barn was just around the corner of the forest patch that cut in throughout the farmland. Back on my feet, I took a step toward the barn and that's when I heard the noise, the faint sound of steel stabbing through the ground.

Someone was digging.

I crept forward, a glow from inside the barn reaching its yellow fingers outward, the rest of my path lit in mystery. Who could be out there now? Shannon was supposed to be picking up Michael from the river, but I hadn't heard back from either of them, and with Laurel in the hospital...no one should be there.

Every bit of debris beneath my feet snapped, the whole while I was trying my damnedest to be quiet. Finally, as I inched closer, the sound of my breath louder than a freight train, I saw a white box. I moved closer, carefully searching for what Ori wanted me to find, eyes flicking to the roof, the windows, to the side stalls...back to the large white box.

I wanted to turn away, to back up with my arms held high above my head like I was trying to scare off a rogue bear, but I couldn't stop analyzing the ninety-degree angles until a memory formed into something familiar. I wasn't sure exactly what I saw, so I walked closer until I could see the object clearer, a white freezer with band stickers on it.

"What the fuck?" It was the freezer at Shannon's. But what was it doing there?

"Johnna?" The voice was shaky...a startled tone.

Shannon was walking out of a dark stall, hands smacking his thighs to brush off dirt. My mind whizzed in all directions, took avenues of every possible scenario, and nothing I came up with made sense.

"Shannon?" I couldn't take my eyes off the freezer. "What are you doing here? Did you find Michael?"

He walked toward me. I backed away, and he stopped. "I couldn't find him."

My eyes dragged down the length of him, dirt-stained Dickies, face smudged in dust and sweat. "What are you doing out here, and why is that here?" I pointed to the freezer, my muscles remembering the hard edges jabbing the back of my thighs. "You fucked me on it!" I yelled.

"It wasn't like that." He shrank. "You weren't supposed to be here. You weren't supposed to *beee here*."

Fire was in my throat. Ori's face burned my vision as I

recalled the words Laurel said at the hospital. "What's in that freezer, Shannon?" Panic took control, sent every muscle into a frenzy of flinching that I couldn't control. Bile rose up my throat while my mind prepared for his answer.

"Nothing." He swallowed hard. "Just go home, Johnna. Please."

A glint of shiny silver caught my attention, and I looked over to see a shovel leaning against the wall, fresh dirt on its spade.

"Who, Shannon?" My heartbeat was in my ears.

He squinted, the hanging work light shading him to a silhouette as he stepped closer. "Please, Johnna. It's not what you think."

"Then what is it?" My eyes darted around for a weapon.

He took another step forward, his boots crunching on old hay that Michael had laid to soak up automotive fluids. But his body language was soft, like he was trying to coax me off a ledge. Only I didn't want to come down. I wanted to jump.

Tears pooled my eyes...fear, anger, rage...all vying for me to buckle under one of them, and just before he got close enough to grab me, I bolted into a nearby stall, slamming the door closed behind me. While he fumbled with the lock, I jumped over the wall into the next stall. The door hinges creaked when he forced open the door and he was over the wall and into the same stall as me so fast I thought he'd teleported. Old feed barrels had been stacked up and when I ran past them, I reached up and gripped the rim of the one on top and pulled them down behind me, buying me enough time to run out of the stall and to the hole behind the freezer, a mound of dirt still waiting to be shoveled back into the ground. But there was nothing in the hole, which meant...

I reached for the freezer lid, flung it open.

"Oh my God!"

CHAPTER TWENTY-SIX

"Nooo!" I screamed, feeling my voice vibrate up my temples. The pressure wanted to crack my skull open, squeeze out through the fissures and leak into the air. "Ori." I sobbed, frozen there, knowing my violent end was coming up fast behind me. There wasn't enough time to process Ori's mangled body. A jolt of urgency bored through me, Ori's voice screaming for me to run, and when Shannon's foot beats alerted me of his dangerous proximity, I ran, not knowing if I'd end up in that freezer with her.

I jumped over the old tractor engine that had been sitting in the bay since we first moved there and ran down the path, hoping like hell I'd make it to the farmhouse in time to lock out Shannon. The barn lights faded, and all I had was my memory of the trail. Shannon didn't have it seared into his mind like I did, so there was a chance. Rain clouds smothered the full moon, and for that I was grateful. The light would have blared a clear view of the path, and he'd have been on me by now.

I reached the back door and slammed it shut, trembling hands fumbling to lock the chain. I rushed into the kitchen, grabbed the phone and dialed 911, reliving the memory of calling for Laurel.

Dispatch answered. "911, what's your emergency?"

"I'm at 1712 Back Road, Sweetwater! Hurry, please!"

"Ma'am, what's your name?"

The back door busted open with a loud bang; he was in the house.

"Hurry! He's going to kill me!" When I saw his shadow near the doorway leading into the kitchen, I dropped the phone and ran, the dispatchers voice still pleading for my name.

In the foyer, a snap decision to run upstairs made me instantly feel like I deserved what I got. Every horror movie shows the victim running upstairs when the front door was right there. But something told me to stay inside. I knew the house, all its hiding spots, like the water pipe access door in my old room. I closed the door as quiet as I could, not sure it was quiet enough, but there was no turning back.

In the time I'd been gone, the room had become a storage space, boxes that contained who knows what shit, and they were all blocking the two foot by two foot door. My heart wanted out, my mind wanted to cut off, but fear drove me, shoving heavy boxes aside like they were full of Styrofoam peanuts. The last stack was heavier than the others and it only moved a few inches. Out in the hallway, the wooden floors cracked and stretched under his weight, and then the noises stopped. He didn't know which room I was in.

"I don't want to hurt you, Johnna. I just want to talk this out." His voice carried down the hall.

Bullshit. Do you think I'm stupid? I tried squeezing through the crack, the slim door digging into my shoulder. I wasn't going to fit. "Fuck," I gritted under my breath. His footsteps drew closer, their shadow beneath the door stopping. There was nowhere for me to go. He was going to find me, and he would kill me when he did.

Lightning cracked outside and lit up the room, drawing my eyes to the window. I jumped up, quiet as I could, and raced over, opening the window. But I wasn't climbing out; I just hoped he'd think I did.

I slinked back to a pile of boxes, slid behind them and waited, holding my breath, praying he couldn't hear my pounding heart. My eyes were trying to keep up from bouts of dark to blinding whites as the storm cracked, but during one of the lightning strikes, I saw the doorknob twist.

A click, a succession of whining creaks...a footstep inside the room. I swallowed, thought the sound of my throat gulping down fear was so loud the drunks at Tantrums could hear it. I peeked at him through a small space made between two stacks, his eyes focused on the open window. Sweat ran into my eyes, burned like hell, but I dared not move to wipe them.

He sighed, and then went to the window, closing it gently. "You don't understand, Johnna." He turned back to the room, old memorabilia and mildew our non-consenting witnesses. "Please, just listen to me."

A whimper pushed behind my lips; my hand slapped over my mouth to stifle it. I bit the back of my finger, the pain keeping me centered. Without it, I'd spiral. I eyed the open door, zero ideas for an escape. My mind was blank.

"I didn't kill Ori, Johnna. It was an accident. She got hit by a car," he said, his throaty voice a bitter icing on crumbling cake.

I looked back to him, his eyes catching me through the small crack, my shadow cast on the wall behind as lightning rolled endlessly.

Fuck! I had no options then, so I ran, slipped out of the door and slammed it shut. The closest room was Michael's. I threw open the door and ran straight to the window, already open, rain carried in by the wind. I crawled out onto the roof as Shannon bolted in. My shoes hit the slick shingles, and I slipped, falling and sliding down. I thrashed at the small risers in between each section, but they were too small to grip and I was airborne.

I opened my eyes, raindrops splashing, making my vision blurry. I gasped, the wind knocked out of me when I hit the ground. "Ungh," I cried, rolling to my side, my cheeks landing on a pair of boots. "No," I pleaded, tears lost in the rain. He rolled me over. I coughed, still trying to catch my breath.

He straddled me, then gently slid his feet down until he was lying on top, his arms on either side of me. Wet tendrils stuck to his forehead, dark eyes staring down. He leaned close, put his lips to my ear. "Why won't you listen to me? I asked you so many times to leave this to me and you just couldn't." Pressure crushed my abdomen, his full weight on me now. His hands slid around my neck and cupped the back of my head. "You are everything to me. I did all of this for you," he cried. Lightning splintered the sky above him.

I kicked and bucked, but he was too heavy, and I was still out of breath from the impact. "Stop!" I gurgled, but my pleas caught in my throat. Pressure clenched my head and pain shot out in all directions, an orb of fire that couldn't be squelched by the pouring rain.

"I don't want to hurt you, Johnna, just calm down!" he begged.

Sirens bled through the rain, and Shannon stood, his head snapping around to the encroaching police cars. He didn't run though. Instead, he pivoted away, and jogged toward them, flagging down the squad car, pointing to me when the officer rolled down their window. "She's hurt real bad!" he yelled over the storm.

My stomach pitched and nausea flushed away what was left of my will, a ringing in my ears so loud I wanted my head to explode. But all I could do was watch Shannon convince his police buds I was unhinged about Laurel and had accidentally hurt myself. It would be an easy lie. A lie fabricated by two decades of town gossip about Laurel and Barrett. These cops would believe anything Shannon told them; my only choice was to stop fighting.

I knew I was dying when I saw Ori over at the pecan tree where she and I used to scour the ground for nuts, filling so many paper bags. She took my hand in hers, both of us sheltered from the storm by sprawling branches thick with a fresh bloom of leaves out of winter. I was painless there with her, a weightlessness I'd never felt. She smiled, leaned in and kissed my cheek. "My sweet sister, you aren't done yet." She backed away, police lights beaming blue across her pale face until she had vanished away.

CHAPTER TWENTY-SEVEN

"Welcome back, Miss LaGrange," a doctor said, dark eyes scanning an open file in her hand, black hair in a perfect bun at the base of her neck. "I'm Dr. Chen." She crossed the room and stood at my bedside, light pen in hand. She clicked it on. "Can you look at me?" She clicked it off. "Okay, follow my finger." I followed right to left and back again. Up then down...all the directions an eye could look. "We're going to get some blood work and run some tests, an EKG and an EEG. If those come back good, we can release you to the CTC."

My brain was mud and I felt like a truck had hit me, so abbreviations weren't cutting it. "CTC?"

"Crisis treatment center. It's policy. Anyone who comes through here because of self-harm goes there for a few days," she said plainly, her pen scratching over the clipboard in her hand. "It's just for observation," she added.

"I don't need observation. I need to talk to my brother." My words slurred and I realized I was still lagging.

Dr. Chen stood straight, hands at her side. "You jumped off a roof." She blinked. "The police are already involved. Nothing you or I can do about that." She took a sharp breath. "Do you remember that? Do you remember jumping?"

I remember Shannon chasing me. "I didn't jump. I fell because—"

"Officer Hager said he watched you jump." The doctor's focus dropped everything and pulled a seat up to my bedside. "Is that inaccurate?"

I was afraid now. I should be dead, or at least paralyzed from the fall, yet I only feel like I have a major hangover. I wanted to tell her the truth, but as the words formed in my throat, I clamped my lips shut. Dr. Chen would no doubt take my statement back to the police, and they would have plenty of time to cover it up before anyone voiced the need for an external investigation. "Ummm, I'm really tired, can I please just rest?"

She gave me a polite, professional smile. "Alright. Someone will be by in a while to check on you." And out the door she went.

I looked down at the gauze taped on the crevice of my elbow. A yellow bracelet that read *fall risk* hung loose on my wrist. The mounted TV was off, the room quiet and the silence only let in choked pleas I remembered as I begged for my life. "Fuck." I stood, less stable than I'd anticipated, and when I wobbled, I grabbed the steel pole to the motoring machine. It squealed its wheels behind me as I crossed the room to the window, the dark outside reflecting my image back to me. Dirt crusted in my hairline, specks of blood dotted my face, and as I reached for the twig in my hair, I laughed. There was nothing at all funny about what had just happened...Shannon, the love of my life, had murdered my sister and tried to murder me, and now everyone thinks I tried to kill myself. Still though, the irony wasn't lost on me.

"What the fuck?" I reached a hand to my face, dragging it along my swollen jawline. Then my fingers found another little tangle of ground debris. I moved my hand down farther to tired, mud-streaked arms, and then my eyes locked on a huge spread of dark purple from my shoulder to my elbow. My heart clenched, ached to fold in on itself, pulse beating in my ears. And all I could think about was how completely mutilated and broken Ori looked in that freezer.

Footsteps behind me, I turned to see the nurse.

"Miss LaGrange, you need to be in the bed. We haven't cleared you for brain trauma. You could fall," Nurse Gonzalez said. She came to my side and ushered me back to bed. I thought about Barrett...how Laurel would have to fight with him some days to get him to stay in the at-home hospital bed. "Now don't worry, a police officer is on their way to ask you a few questions, but after that you can rest," the nurse said, tucking the sheet under my legs and patting my foot once the task was finished.

This was bad. Did she mean Shannon? "Who?"

"Excuse me?" she asked, pressing buttons on the machines above my head.

"Which police officer is coming?"

My body flashed hot. I wasn't at the county hospital. They'd taken me to Cape Fear General, the hospital closest to home. I guess they thought I really was about to die.

"Oh, I'm not sure." She smiled, then turned her gaze to the equipment.

I had to get out of there. "Um, I'm feeling nauseous. Could I please have some ginger ale or Sprite?"

"Sure thing. I'll be right back." Night shifts were usually low staffed which was good for me. I waited a few seconds for the nurse to be far enough away that once I ripped myself free, I'd have time to run before she could get to my room.

I dug my nails under the sticky pads on my chest and started tearing them off, bitching stings every one of them. Next was the IV. I thought adrenaline would mask the grotesque sensation of pulling a PICC line out of my veins, but it didn't. I grimaced as the worms slithered beneath my skin; my stomach ready to send anything upward in revolt.

I ran for the door, pressed my ear close, listening for the sign of a clean break. I cracked it open, straining to see down the hallway, my eyes landing on an abandoned custodian's cart. Eager, ready to be free and get to Michael, I popped my head out, getting a full view down both ends of the hallway. All the way to the elevator.

The coast is clear.

I slipped out of the room and darted toward the elevator. It was so close. Closer than I'd expect an elevator to have been to a patient's room with all the noise that came with elevator cargo. Crying babies, bratty kids, inconsolable parents and loved ones. I was in the critical care unit, after all. I pressed my finger onto the cool, silver-plated elevator button, the down arrow lighting up, chewing a thin line of skin off the inside of my bottom lip while I waited. Anxiety was a bitch.

Ding. The telltale sound of an elevator about to open its mouth. I looked up, metal doors reflecting my trembling image, when the doors spread open.

And there he was.

"Shannon!" I gasped.

His face twisted in confusion.

I heard my heartbeat in my ears. If Shannon got his arms around me, I'd never escape, and he'd try to kill me all over again.

I pivoted, pushed off the wall with my hands and sprinted toward the stairwell. My feet smacked the floor in little thuds that made me miss my favorite pair of Vans. But my coordination was off, and my legs were confused and I busted my ass right in the middle of my getaway. The side of my head slapped the floor, and I froze in pain, sterile white walls spinning.

But then spite kicked in, and I pulled myself back up, Shannon an arm's length away. I ran again, reaching the stairwell, flinging open the door and reveling in the thought of smacking Shannon in the face with it; he was so close. I wanted to turn and look back at him, see exactly how close he really was, but I needed to keep running.

I leapt the stairs by threes, off center and wonky, like some jacked-up slinky. But I was still upright and keeping distance from Shannon.

When I turned the flight leading to the next level, I braved a glance upward, Shannon too close for me to outrun him once we reached a straight away. *Damn he's fast.*

Maybe I could lose him on the next floor? At the next access door, I threw my body into it to keep momentum, pushing it open and bursting down the hall on the hospital's second level. My hair whipped behind me in matted tendrils, the hospital gown coming loose from its barely tied bonds.

I snapped my head around, Shannon coming through the door before it even started closing. On my left was a room, but it faced toward the hospital's interior, so I darted into the room on the right, its door wide open. In the room a nurse was messing with a machine that swung off the wall above the empty patient bed. She turned at the noise of me crashing in, eyes wide, scanning every inch of me.

"Honey, where do you belong? Are you okay?" I froze, like she had a gun pointed.

Just then, Shannon barged in, breathing like he did when we'd gone a second round in bed. The memory of us together tickled my stomach. "No," I started, moving slowly toward the window and away from him. "That's my boyfriend. He's why

I'm in here. I know he's a cop, but he's a dick. He's going to hurt me."

Shannon held up his hands. "I'm not going to hurt anybody."

The woman kept her distance from me, but moved between us, shielding me from him. "Sir, I don't know who you are, but you need to leave. She's obviously a patient here, and my concern is for her."

"I'm officer Shannon Hager. This woman is in here for self-harm." He eyed the nurse, then snapped his sight back to me.

She turned to me, "Honey, I need you to tell me your name." Her voice was calm, but her eyes were focused, and I noticed movement, the woman's hand raising to a blue button above the empty bed. "I've sent out a code, so in about ten seconds this room will be flooded with doctors and nurses and all kinds of people that will want to know what's going on here." Her eyes flicked to Shannon, likely searching for a sign that he understood and wouldn't come any closer.

It came to me how scary it must be for the woman to be in a room with an armed police officer and a patient who might be suicidal...both yelling at her to listen.

But help was coming and if they caught me, Shannon would have a lot of time to pin all this on me, or worse, Michael. *Shit.*

Light from the full moon slipped in through the window and cast my shadow on the wall across the room. Looking out, I counted windows on the adjoining building and knew I was on the second floor then.

I have to jump.

It was my only way out and would hurt like hell. Solar lights dotted the landscape, and I could see the ground was a steep hill, ornamental shrubs and flowers spread out, just all in my way, and if I were lucky, I'd land in a way that I could buckle and roll, like in those movies where the main character falls from a helicopter but lands on a sand dune and just rolls up like one of those little gray bugs.

It was the only way I'd leave the hospital and find Michael. I would never get past Shannon or a hoard of medical staff. It wasn't happening. But the glass was thick, tempered to withstand hurricanes. How the hell was I supposed to break it? I searched the room. There was a chair for waiting family members an arm's length away, but that arm's length was a movement closer to Shannon. *What the fuck am I going to do?*

I turned back to the nurse, her eyes locked on Shannon's like he was some snake all coiled and ready to strike. Next to Nurse Mamma Bear was a drip bag holder, nice metal tip. Without another thought, I snatched it and smashed the window. It shattered like that delicious red candy on an apple. But that's what you get from hospitals in low-income areas. Old ass windows. No funding. Shit politicians who couldn't care less.

I took a split second to scan the only two people who could stop me, both still facing away from the splintering glass, their hands instinctively covering their faces from sharp fragments that went flying. Now was my chance.

So, I jumped.

CHAPTER TWENTY-EIGHT

My feet slapped wet grass, and I buckled. But I didn't roll into a ball. Instead, my body thrashed down the hill like a pair of open scissors thrown across the room in anger. A blinding pain cracked through my body. The world shifted from ground to sky to ground and back again, my throat burning with stomach acid, chest palpitating. I had to break my descent. A branch or root or boundary fencing, I just needed something to grab hold to. I flailed a hand out, snatched something solid and yelled in pain as the object cut through my palm, forcing my hand off.

I focused, cradled my head with my arms when the ground came, flung out my hands to reach for anything while I was upright, and finally, after so many cartwheels down the steep embankment, I slammed against a tree, and everything stopped.

I opened my eyes to darkness, my mouth wide as I gasped for air. I rolled on the ground, beat my chest until finally I gasped, drawing in desperate breaths.

Time was precious though, and there was no time for recovery. I scanned the area, an irrigation pond to my left, the hospital to my right. At the back of the irrigation pond, a dark spot caught my eye. Distant streetlights couldn't reach the depths of the drainage pipe but showed me enough of what it was.

I pushed off from the tree and staggered toward it, each step a little less painful than the last, a little more coordinated. I crawled through the drainpipe, muddy stink squishing up and around my toes. When I poked out my head, I was across from the main street that ran alongside the hospital. A city bus squeaked to a stop. If I hurried, I could catch it. The street was coming alive with early morning work traffic and was wet from the storm, a feather's touch drizzle still falling. I ran, rounding the front of the bus, its doors open, welcoming me in.

"You getting on or what, lady? I don't have all night." The bus driver scowled, lips pursed. Then she drew her eyes over me, noticing the hospital gown. "You okay?"

"I, uh..." The shop door behind me creaked open, a bell anchored above it ringing, the shop owner a thin woman with graying hair smelling of coffee and syrup clumsily chalking on a street sign advertisement: *Hot coffee and waffles $3.99 for the early crowd.* "I'm fine."

I turned around and ran into the cafe, never mind that the owner was outside writing on the chalkboard sign. But her eyes stayed on me, because everyone in their right mind knew it wasn't right for someone in a hospital gown to be running the streets. The woman scribbled the last word, her expression set on dousing me with a hundred questions. I spun around, bumping into the worn wooden checkout counter, my fingers knocking over a mason jar of pens topped with fake flowers, and then I noticed the red exit sign. I ran toward it, hoping like hell it would pop open and spit me out into a back alley. My palms slammed against the metal push bar, a beeping sound announcing the door opening. I stumbled out into the alley, steam rising off the walkway.

I wasn't familiar with this area, so any direction I took could lead me to a dead end or worse, Shannon. I needed to get my bearings, find someplace safe to hide out until I could come up with a plan, which seemed like an unreachable goal right now. I desperately scanned the area, a dumpster and storage shack sat across from the alleyway, but behind them was a small patch of trees...at least in there I wouldn't be out in the open. I pushed through the trees and stopped abruptly against a chain-link fence slotted with wooden strips for privacy. There must be businesses or housing on the other side; why else would this be here? I followed the length of the fence. It couldn't run on forever, fences never did. But the trees started to dwindle until they were gone, and the end of the fence appeared, the safety of the trees ending with it. I scanned the adjacent parking lot. Shannon wasn't stupid...he'd have officers at the next bus stop, and he'd probably be on foot right now, tearing through the cafe same as I had.

Before I rounded the fence, pain gripped my head, an immobilizing fist squeezing tight. I dropped to my knees, the streetlights a white flash of unbearable bright pain. I shouldn't have screamed. I could have just given away my location, but the pain was so intense, my body in complete control over my brain. I threw my hands over my eyes, hoping to shield some of the light, and when I did, flashes of a dark night intruded, hot and humid, a deep voice, somewhere near but still far off somehow.

Tears burned my cheeks. I didn't know what I was seeing, but I knew it was related to Ori's murder, but why was I seeing and hearing these things? I hadn't had any drugs in over twenty-four hours; I couldn't be hallucinating. I had to snap out of this. Someone was going to see me if I didn't. I tried to stand, but the vision had hold of me still, mighty claws around my ankles, pulling me deeper in.

"No!" My fingers latched through the chain-link, and I pulled myself up, hedgerows and the faint yelps of an alley dog smothering the memory. I looked around, another fence just a few feet away partitioning a neighborhood from the strip mall, a row of worn wooden privacy panels. I leaned forward and looked through the slats at the remnants of a back yard party, a big black dog lying on a covered porch waiting out the rain. String-lights bobbled in the wind. The last weather forecast I remembered was a hurricane in the gulf. It must have pushed its way northeast.

In the yard next door, a clothesline strung with sheets and pillowcases flapped. They wouldn't do any better than what I wore now, so a quick snatch and run wouldn't work. "I just need some clothes." I slipped behind a dumpster, feeling time crushing in. Shannon would be close behind...but there were a few storefronts opening. He'd sweep through 'em fast. Across the strip mall parking lot, a car rattled to a stop, a loud bang as an old man driving cut off the engine. I whipped my head around, no one but me and...

"Let me get that." I stepped in front of the frail old man, a laundry basket buried in his chest, and opened the door to the 24-hour laundromat. Inside, a dryer turned over a colorful load. I walked toward it, hoping it'd be actual clothes, but caught a bright green sock spin by. A tiny green sock. Followed by a tiny bib and what looked like a onesie with dinosaurs on it, pinned to the clear glass by an oversized load.

"Great, baby clothes." I turned back to the old man, arms shaking as he stretched out to lift the load on top the Formica counter, edges peeling back to worn particle board, coffee rings staining the top. He abandoned the basket, trembling fingers thumbing to open his wallet, going for the change machine on the back wall. All the time in the world just fell in my lap. I grabbed the basket, pulled it closer, begrudgingly lifted a few pair of boxer briefs aside. "These will do." I pulled out a pair of khaki shorts and a white T-shirt.

Slinking away to the restroom, hoping I could change and bolt before the old man made it back. "You're a real asshole, Johnna," I chided myself, bursting through the bathroom door while stripping off the hospital gown. I let it fall to the ground, hopped into the shorts, then pulled over the wrinkled T-shirt. It didn't make any of this better that I didn't know the old man. I could never get money to him to replace the items. I snatched up the hospital gown, crumpled it and tossed it in the trash then tugged open the bathroom door, a smooth quiet whoosh as its rubber bottom trim passed over the slick tile.

But the old man was back and sorting out his laundry on the table. I couldn't leave without him seeing me, and maybe I didn't deserve to get away without that real gut punch that comes with being caught. Top that with some guilt and you've got yourself a great, towering shit cake, and I was eating the biggest slice.

He looked up from a pair of clouding glasses, watching as I stood there with his clothes on. "I'm sor—"

"What are you running from?" His eyebrows lifted in the center, a sincere tone of concern in his voice.

I wanted to say something that didn't sound crazy, but I had nothing because all this was insane. I was almost murdered by a guy I'd trusted completely, and now I was on the run. "The police." It was a logical and truthful answer; he at least deserved some honesty since I stole his shorts and shirt.

"I didn't ask who. I asked *what?*"

Same thing, right? "I don't know," I said, feebly. This man was looking inside me, and I felt every bit of it.

He sniffed, looked back down at his clothes. "Well, whatever it is, you're gonna show up looking slick." He smiled a tender smile, like a grandpa wiping dirt off a road rash and telling you it'll be okay. My grandpa never smiled, and he certainly wouldn't care to brush off a booboo. In any case, the man was letting me leave with his belongings, and I could never repay him.

"Thanks." I pushed open the door into the rainy night, pavement fumes flitting up in pungent streams.

Sweetwater proper wasn't that far, but morning had come and hiding would be much harder. It felt safe in the dark, like my escaping police custody would stay hidden as long as there was no light to shine on the crime.

Looking down at my toes, I thought about a summer when all I did was play outside barefoot, running in the woods with Michael behind an abandoned train lot. Laurel didn't like us playing there, but it had the best hiding places for hide-n-go-seek, and we were always finding cool bottles that had been thrown out by workers from back in the forties and fifties. That summer though, I'd worn through my school sneakers and Laurel refused to buy me new ones until the school year started even though she had money—Barrett's money—to get me a new pair, so I went barefoot. Me and Michael had just started our game—Michael was hiding—and I was searching when I stepped on a broken glass bottle and nearly cut off my pinky toe. Not only did I get a whoopin' for disobeying Laurel, I got an infection that took my toe because the horse penicillin Laurel gave me didn't work.

Sweetwater was close, but what the hell was I going to do once I got there? Going to the farmhouse was out of the question. The police would be there. *Shannon* might be there, and I didn't have a plan yet. There was no one to call...Michael was MIA and Laurel was dead for all I knew.

A car zipped by, horn blasting. I jumped back, instinct pulling me to hide, tripped over the combination of cement and dirt on the roadside and fell to my knees, palms splayed out on the ground. "Asshole!" I shouted, watching the car shrink into the horizon. I brushed off my knees and wiped my hands against each other, careful not to purposefully soil the clothes I borrowed—*you stole*—from the nice man at the laundromat. I just needed time and a safe place to hide out until I could dye my hair and find some clothes that actually fit.

The hairs on the back of my neck stood, skin prickling, the feeling of eyes watching, weird and threatening...a survival mechanism kicking in. I turned around, catching the faint white line spreading wider in the darkness. Another car. But not just any car. It was a cop, lights flashing red and blue off the trees.

I ran into the pines lining both sides of Route 9, careful not to go too far in on account of all the rain spilling the swamps closer to the road. I stood behind a pine to watch as the car passed, reflective Horry County decal whizzing by in a blue and white streak, the squad number 574 barely catching my eye. "Shannon."

The flashing red light at Sweetwater's intersection on Main Street was a beacon through the trees. *Well, here I am. Now what? I can't go home. I have no phone.* It's funny how reliant we are on the convenience of our cell phones. How everyone was just a touch away from contact. Until they're not.

The wet street reflected bright lights off the telephone poles, the lit diners and shops, the yellows and reds from the gas station. I scoped the parking lot, one car sitting at a pump, its driver at the register inside. "Gabe."

I tiptoed out of the cover of so many pines, checked for cars, and ran across the dark intersection, slipping behind the streetlights lining Main Street. My feet splashed in puddles as I ran, droplets of water splattering up the backs of my legs. I felt like a kid and a criminal all at the same time, which was really fucked up.

The smell of charcoaled meat filled my nose. I passed behind Pattie's, the local hamburger joint that had provided dinner more times than I could count. The best strawberry shake around, and fries so salty and crisp. I'd kill to have a basket right now.

Just let it happen, Johnna. Kimber's voice rang in my ears. I stopped running, grabbed the gutter railing along the corner of the brick building, pain blinding me, knocking me off balance. The sharp memory spread across my skull, pounded in my temples, and raged down my neck. Tears pooled in my eyes.

I'm not going to prison for ya'll bitches. Kimber's voice was flat, Ori's death an inconvenience. I tried to compartmentalize the pain, squash it into the hollow spaces inside; there were so many now.

CHAPTER TWENTY-NINE

Each vision of Ori's death hit me harder and harder. The only difference now was a sense of urgency, but I didn't know what that meant. Ori was already dead, but the visions were getting worse, like a squatter movie that wouldn't leave even if I waved an eviction letter in my hand.

I felt close to her in a way I'd never been before. That had to mean something. It had to mean that she wants me to bring her murderers to justice. At least in the afterlife she trusted me to help her, and I wasn't about to let her down.

I shook away the pain. Gabe was still in the store, and when he flicked his head to the rack of cigarettes behind the counter, I knew there was still time.

His Jeep was at the gas pump closest to the station, so I had to be careful as I slinked across the lot and up to the hatch of his rusting Wrangler. Popping my head up to catch a glimpse of him again, I stayed hunkered and opened the back passenger door facing the pump, slipping inside without being seen. A small victory. I'd take any success I could get.

Slouching in the backseat, my heart pumped faster as shoe soles scratched across the lot, closer and closer. The Jeep bounced when he got inside, and I waited for him to start it up and drive off before popping out.

"Gabe, it's Johnna," I said, rising slowly...trying my best not to freak him out.

"Holy shit!" He swerved and I fell into the backseat. The tires squealed, rubber chirping over wet pavement and he pulled over in the middle of Main Street. Exactly what I didn't want him to do.

"Gabe," I sat back up, looking at him as he glared at me with giant eyes. "Please keep driving. We need to talk."

"No! Fuck no! Get out of my car." He flew out of the Jeep and flung open the back door. "Out."

"Please. I have nowhere else to go."

He wasn't fazed. "The cops are looking for you. They're saying you escaped the hospital." He pushed his palm against his forehead, stress or fear steering his movements. "It's all over the news. Some people are saying you had something to do with Ori's murder."

I wasn't sure how Shannon spun it, but I knew it had to be good because he fooled me, and I thought I'd perfected my bullshit detector since I depended on it for survival. "I didn't kill my fucking sister."

The night was lifting, the silver slit of dawn threatening my cover. I needed to get somewhere private.

"I'm on my way to work, Johnna. I don't have time for this."

"Please, Gabe. If it weren't for me the cops would still be sniffing up your ass. You owe me." He didn't owe me shit, but I had no cards left...nothing to rely on except his curiosity to hear me out.

He sniffed, looked at his phone for the time and squeezed his eyes shut in what seemed to be an inner battle with himself. "Goddamnit." He got in the Jeep and turned around, heading back to his house. "I'm going to be late for work, so this better be good."

I lay on his back seat and told him what I'd seen Shannon doing at the Farmhouse with Ori's body. I didn't hold back when I described Shannon's attempt at murdering me. "He tried to kill me."

Gabe was silent, his eyes searching for something in the air that wasn't there, something to make sense of what I'd just said, until finally he snapped to life. "So if he tried to kill you, then why did he let you go to the hospital?"

That was a great question, and I didn't know how to answer because it made me sound crazy. But I tried. "I don't know. Maybe he hoped he could finish me off once he got to the hospital?" I lifted my head to see Gabe's reaction...if he bought my shit.

He nodded. "Okay, so what are you going to do?"

"You believe me then?" I needed an ally. I needed his trust.

"I don't know what to believe, but I do know them Hager boys have done some awful shit and Shannon always turned his eye." He turned and glanced at me. "He fooled you. The smartest chick in the world according to Ori."

I couldn't help but laugh. The sentiment wasn't new; Ori had said those exact words to me so many times. I was smart for leaving and getting a great job and making a life for myself in the big city. If she only knew how shitty it all turned out. "Yeah, well, we all fall down." Only I fell fucking hard and fast with no safety net...headfirst into Shannon's endless pit of deception.

We pulled up to Gabe's house, and I got out. He reached out his car window and fumbled with his key chain. "Here"—he slid a key off a large key ring—"take this."

"Thank you." I took it, a passing thought of wondering had Ori used it before?

"Just stay inside until I get back. I don't want no one seeing you here."

I nodded, shrank at the reality that had me pegged as the bad guy. "Sure, of course."

"Feel free to shower and eat whatever you find. Not a whole lot besides ramen and beer, but...okay then." He started his Jeep and waited for me to get inside the house, his eyes on my back sending an uncomfortable unease down my neck. It was only a few days ago when I thought he was the reason Ori was gone, and now I was hiding out in his house, depending on him to keep from being caught. At least for now.

I was attacked by a pack of dogs when I was seven. Me and Michael in a circle of teeth and fur. Laurel got him out, took off runnin' for the house while the mutts dug into my skin. A shotgun scared them off later, so I'm told, but I'd blacked out before all the savin' happened. My granny said I'd been blessed, that the attack was a gift. The dogs had chosen me as their mantle, a crowning in the afterlife. I'd never understood it, but it was all I had to help me cope with the trauma as a kid. Not so much the dog part, but the part of my mother leaving me. I'd take a hundred teeth over the feeling of being left to die alone.

I stared at the ceiling, heart beating out of my chest like it did every time I woke up. And just like clockwork, I reached for my arm, for the scars left behind by old wounds. No need to turn to look at it; I knew the scars were still there. Can't dream those away.

"You okay?" Gabe asked, standing in the doorway, beer in hand. I'd dozed off and hadn't heard him come home.

I stared at the gold flecks glinting in the ceiling. "I'm fine." I rubbed my eyes, reached for the glass of water on the end table. "I really slept through your entire shift?"

He shook his head. "No. I got off work early. Told the boss I had to go to the station and talk to the cops again. They've been hassling me so much it wasn't a stretch for him to believe me."

I rolled my shoulders back, a pop in my upper back releasing the stress of these last few days. Gabe slid a pile of comics books off the couch seat and sat next to me. "So, what are you going to do?"

The only thing I could do. "I have to find Ori's body and prove they killed her."

He tilted his chin up and chugged the beer. "How are you going to do that?" He let out a controlled, respectable belch...if such a thing existed.

"I don't know yet, but I need to warn Michael, and he's at the river."

"For all you know, your brother could have killed Kimber and Jamie."

What the fuck did he just say? I tasted the sour sting of blood as I bit down on my lip. But before I shouted, the possibility of Michael killing the Hager brothers settled around me like a blanket fresh from the dryer. If I knew the brothers were connected to Ori's murder, Michael could know too. Maybe that's why he'd been trying to rush me out of Sweetwater. He could get away with a lot more if I weren't around.

As if I'd forgotten the last few days—Kimber trying to kill me; waking in Ori's bed covered in dirt and blood, I said, "Well, he did the world a favor then."

Gabe raised his eyebrows, took another cigarette from the pack and bit it between his teeth. "You ain't takin' my Jeep." The raw flick of a lighter flint cracked.

"You're going to make me walk? That would take a lot of

time. Precious time. Time we could be spending trying to catch that asshole."

His eyebrows screwed inward. "I'll do it for Ori, but once we get to the river, you're on your own. I can't get caught up in all this."

Some boyfriend. "Fine."

In his Jeep, the music low...loud enough to hear the song playing, a drop D guitar riff and rolling double kick base, I churned my memories for anything I could do to prove that Shannon killed Ori. Flickers of a night she might have died wouldn't cut it. I needed hard evidence but had jack shit.

I rolled down the window, let the night air hit my face. I smelled a hint of salt, the storm drawing sea water so nearby. Ori was going to be a mother; she would've been great at it. My heart cramped, the pain a dense weight pulling my organs inward on each other. I looked over at Gabe, his eyes locked on the road ahead, drizzle blurring his bug-splattered windshield. He knew Ori was pregnant and was pretty sure it wasn't his, but even that donkey kick to the balls wasn't enough to stop him from loving her, which he still did. I saw on his face, clear as a spit-shined shot glass.

CHAPTER THIRTY

I had no way to see the path leading to Wilford's Cliff, so I followed the sounds of a small crowd that was gathered at the top. Gabe drove off as soon as I stepped down from his Jeep, a slight wave goodbye. I didn't blame him for staying out of this mess, especially since he was already on probation, but a spine goes a long way in these parts.

I walked with my arms outstretched. The last thing I needed was a busted nose from a giant pine. "Michael," I yelled, hoping he'd hear me and find me halfway up the path. The voices shifted cadence from a casual rhythm to a tone of question. I chuckled at the thought of having scared the shit out of a bunch of paranoid dope heads. "Michael!"

Footsteps slapped the muddy ground. "Johnna?"

"Michael. I'm over here." A penlight caught my eyes through the trees. "Here!" I waved my hands, and I could tell he saw me when the penlight stopped on my shirt.

"What are you doing out here?" He rubbed his cheek on his shoulder, itching at a mosquito bite.

I pulled him toward me. "We need to go. Where is your car?"

"What's going on?" His expression was precise...sincere, so whatever drugs he'd been taking were out of his system.

"Laurel's in the hospital."

"What? Why?"

I grabbed his hand in comfort. "I don't know Michael. But she's bad."

"Fuck!" He started banging his phone on his head like some psycho out of a Stephen King movie. He bolted through the trees, heading back to his camp. I followed, knowing he was grabbing his shit so we could go.

He was quiet the whole time, hurriedly shoving a sleeping bag into its nylon bag. "Krista, can you bring the rest of my things when y'all leave?" A pretty girl with curly brown hair and freckles nodded.

We were on the move again and once we got to his car, he flung open the trunk and triggered another vision in me. Screams, husky and shrill and from more people than I could clarify. Blurred images of windshield wipers smearing rain and red across the glass, and before I could get my bearings, I heard my brother ask, "Johnna...you okay?"

I wanted to answer, but my words were hung neatly in my mind's closet, my soul trying to make a picture. It was always the same, the pain, blacking out, the blinding white that stole my vision and replaced it with images of swamp and blood and all the horrible things that accompany murder...screams, guttural gasps, the nauseating buzz of fear crawling over my skin.

My body went limp, the memory too much, but as I fell, Michael scooped in and caught me, and then I lost myself.

I woke to the roar of a speeding engine and air battering my face. My eyes rolled until they landed on Michael.

"Puke out if you need to."

I nodded a thank you and turned my chin to rest it on the windowsill. Controlling my breaths was key to keeping the contents of my stomach inside. Slow, steady breaths, controlled in and out again and again until the feeling passed. I brought my self-upright, watched the headlights on the road for a minute before I said, "Shannon killed Ori." The words choked me when they came out and I paused, waited for him to speak, and when he didn't, I added, "He tried to kill me."

His brows pushed downward. "He wouldn't do that, Johnna."

The hell he wouldn't. "I was in the hospital from injuries *he* gave me." I proffered my wrist, exposing a medical band with my name and the date on it along with a fucked-up mosaic of scrapes and cuts, dried blood.

My brother's face went pale. "Are you sure it was him?"

"Yes, I'm sure, Michael." Eager for him to hop on the *Shannon's a murderer* train with me, I said, "He's trying to frame you?"

He lifted a cigarette to his lips, bit it between his teeth while he patted his short pockets for his lighter.

"He had Ori's body in his freezer. I caught him in the barn at the farmhouse, hole dug, her body..." I drifted; the thought of my dead sister being desecrated sent bile up my throat. I swallowed. "He thought I was dead when I fell off the roof, but..." I gestured with my hands to the obvious existence of myself.

At first, I thought he didn't hear me, a blank look on his face as his foot sank heavier on the gas pedal. "Michael?"

He snapped a glance at me. "Why would he kill Ori then move her to our barn?"

My body flushed hot. He thought I was full of shit. I drew my hand to my throat, felt my resolve slide down. "Why don't you believe me?"

He flexed his fingers around the wheel, bit on his bottom lip like it was a Jolly Rancher.

I wanted him to listen. To respond. To act like I just told him I was almost killed by the same person who killed our little sister. "Michael!"

"Fuck, Johnna, let me think!" Spit sprayed from his mouth and his unlit cigarette fell onto his lap.

The only thing I wanted to think about was how to prove Shannon killed Ori. And Jamie. And Kimber. "Just go to the barn, Michael. You'll see. Even if he covered up everything, you'll be able to tell the dirt was disturbed. You know every inch of that place like the inside label of a Jack Daniels bottle."

He pressed his foot down harder and tore through the night to the farmhouse.

CHAPTER THIRTY-ONE

"We can't just kill him, Michael."

He was hyper-focused on the road. "Why not? Doesn't he deserve it? He killed our sister. Tried to kill you. This world will be better off without him."

Michael wasn't wrong, but I wasn't ready to turn my brother into a murderer. That feeling ebbed every time I swallowed and was reminded of Shannon's hands around my throat.

Could I really let Michael do this?

We've kept secrets before. Secrets of murder. And Michael proved he can keep his mouth shut.

"He does deserve it, but—"

"We will never prove that he had anything to do with Ori's murder. By now he's gotten rid of every shred of evidence. I mean...he's a cop for fuck's sake. He knows how to cover this kind of shit up if it needs covering," Michael said.

Shannon would try to cover his tracks, but no one was good enough to make up a story debunking what I could tell the police. "He dug a hole in our barn for fuck's sake. He shot her for fuck's sake. There's bullet forensics, ya know?"

"Easy," Michael said, way too quickly. "He's already told

the police about me, given them a lot of good shit, I'm sure. Their sights will be so focused on me that anything you say will sound like you're covering for me. That department worships him. They'll never believe us."

Fuck fuck fuck fuck. "Fuck!" I didn't want to believe him, but I knew he was right. This town has treated Shannon like some fucking superhero ever since he was in high school and took the football team to state conference every year. But as the pieces of the night Ori was killed tried to make a picture, I couldn't understand one thing. "Why does Shannon think he can frame you?"

"What?" Michael's face flitted from me to the road and back again and again.

I combed my fingers through my hair, irritated by the strands stuck to my face. "I can't understand how he thinks that could even work. You have an alibi for this entire weekend."

Michael was silent, and when he didn't speak my mind began creating its own absurd answers.

"I don't know," he said, finally, a fresh cigarette in his mouth now.

"It doesn't make any sense. If him and his brothers were involved, how could he point any of this at you?" I hadn't spoken to Michael in a long time and certainly wasn't clued in on his life, but I knew that he would never hurt Ori, so the reason Shannon would have to try and frame Michael didn't matter.

"He's desperate," Michael said, smoke spilling from his lips.

Could be. Desperate people take dumb risks and make worse decisions. Jamie and Kimber were killed, so pinning it on them wouldn't go far, and since Michael was close friends with Jamie—they basically hung out 24/7—then it could benefit Shannon somehow to bring up Michael as a prime suspect. "We need a plan. We don't even know where he is."

I winced as a searing pain jousted my temple. "I can guess where he is."

He inhaled the cigarette. "Where?"

"The only place he could ensure the privacy to hide a body."

I could see Michael thinking. "The salvage lot." Michael had a confidence to him that made me proud. Finally he was acting like a big brother whose little sister was murdered and not a hot-head teen going through their emo phase trying to pretend nothing ever happened. He tore through a gravel lot and turned the car around and toward the salvage yard.

We parked a half mile down from the garage so we could use the woods for cover. Before exiting the car I asked, "You got any food from camping in your backpack?"

He gave me a quizzical look. "Yeah. Why?" He reached for his pack and pulled it up to his lap from the back floorboard.

"We've got a junkyard mutt to distract."

He pulled out a pack of jerky.

"That'll work," I said, snatching it from him.

The loneliness I'd felt walking through the woods alone on my way back from the hospital was gone. I had my little brother with me now, and that was all I needed to make it through this nightmare. Me and Michael were always a good team, trapping fish in the river, catching wild rabbits together, we had been so in sync with each other as kids. I hoped we still were.

"So how bad is Mom?" Michael whispered, a genuine concern in his tone.

I hated telling him the truth, but that's all I had. "Pretty bad. I don't think she's going to make it."

He hung his head, and I watched as tears leapt off his chin onto his legs.

I doubted that Laurel was still alive. And part of me hoped she was already gone. Michael didn't need to see her the way I'd seen her, all creepy and possessed like in some scary movie. No one should see their mom like that. So why did I have to?

We reached the garage and my first task was to locate the dog. That fucker would give us away with one sniff of our human stink, so I opened the jerky and pulled out some pieces, fanning them in the air to hide our smell. It was a long shot and probably didn't make any sense, but I wanted to surprise Shannon. I had Michael's phone ready to record his ass. We just needed to get close enough to catch him.

Along the fence line that wrapped into the woods, Michael and I pushed small bits of jerky through the chain-link. We walked as much of the perimeter that we could, all the parts that kept us hidden. Once the pack was empty, we waited to see of the dog would pick up the scent. Once he did, he'd be busy following the breadcrumbs until they were gone. It'd buy us a little bit of time. Hopefully it would be enough.

We crouched near a tree, the moonlight peeking through a clouded night sky. The bad weather was finally moving out and part of me found relief. Like the storms had been an usher for all this madness and with it leaving it might be taking the bad shit with it.

I could only hope.

I craned around the brush to get a better view of the garage. "Shannon's truck is here." I was vibrating with nervousness.

"There's the dog," Michael whispered, pointing to the brown mutt sniffing the fence line about a hundred feet away.

"Good. Let's go." I stood, still crouching and we ran to the back side of the garage. We climbed the fence, every clank and whine of the metal chain links under our weight made my heart stop, and when my shoes hit dirt on the other side, I felt a small victory. "Well, the easy part is over. Now what?"

Michael lifted his shirt, gunmetal flashing under the full moon. "This is *what*."

CHAPTER THIRTY-TWO

Shannon deserved to die. That's what I kept telling myself as we crept closer to the sound of a shovel spade splitting dirt. He killed Ori, stuffed her in a freezer and thought nothing of it.

I was sick. My stomach wanted to lurch until I was sucked into its massive vacuum and vomited up.

But I'd killed before, and the guilt of having suffocated my stepfather while he was incapacitated had scratched at my bones every day since then. And he deserved it. He was dying anyway, but did that really matter? I didn't want Michael to suffer the weight of murder; he'd already lost his sister and likely his mother, so the least I could do was remove that burden.

"Give me the gun," I whispered.

"No. Why?" he rebutted.

I held out my hand. "You know why."

He stared at me for a moment, his eyes locked on confusion, and when that look relaxed, I knew he knew why. "Johnna, just because you got your own justice before won't make this easier for you."

"I can't let you do it." My legs were shaking and the thought of him arguing against the idea made things worse. I just needed him to agree so we could get this over with.

"That asshole killed Ori then he tried to kill you. How in the hell do you think I could feel bad for offing that bitch?"

My guts flipped. He wasn't giving up. "Fine. Just be careful and remember...when you pull the gun, you better use it. Shannon has to be caught off guard or we're going to end up in that hole with Ori."

He nodded, pulled the gun and started toward Shannon. We saw him now and I froze, my mouth dry, palms sweaty, mind circling a freshly cleared drain. This was it.

"Shannon!" Michael boasted, his deep voice more threatening than I'd remembered. But at the announcement, Shannon's hand flinched to his gun belt. My stomach dropped as he pulled his weapon and shot Michael, hitting him in the shoulder. My brother's gun flew out of his hand to the ground next to me.

"Michael!" I watched him fall, his head smacking the ground and bouncing. My eyes darted to the gun, and with an instinct to survive, I dove for it.

A weight on my back knocked me face down on the ground...pressure building in my neck as Shannon's full body landed on me. It was the attack at the farmhouse all over again. I wasn't strong enough to roll over, and when I reached my free hand for the gun, his longer reach clenched it first and threw it behind me where I couldn't see.

"Shannon," I coughed, my ears buzzing, pressure in my temples pushing out.

He flipped me over and in the same motion jammed his gun barrel into my chest. "Fuuuuck Johnna, why are you doing this!" he screamed, eyes bulging, veins popping along his temples.

I heard every mechanism inside the weapon as his finger

squeezed down on the trigger. My ears hissed, my skin pricking in a frenzy to warm itself. I was about to die and my mind was trying to power off. But there was nothing except the weight of Shannon on top of me, his gun pointed to the sky. "I killed Kimber for you! For Jamie!" he sobbed.

Before I could scream, another shot rang out. Shannon's body quaked and he looked down at me, blood spreading across his shirt. "I'm so sorry, Johnna," he spat, blood oozing from his mouth.

"Get off me!" I reached up and yanked his arm, pulling him down to the ground beside me, his body limp...slapping the dirt with a thud that split my mind in half.

He was gone.

Just like that.

I took my time standing, my battered bones fighting me every step of the way, but there I was, hovering over Shannon's corpse, the fear he incited in me still beating at the underside of my skin, screaming to get out.

The stark silence made me dizzy, but grunts of pain zeroed in everything. "Michael!"

I rushed to his side, helping him sit up, ignoring the slight whimper in his voice because it was breaking my heart. "Give me the gun." I gently took the weapon, its weight pulling my hand down.

"I'm okay," he grumbled, wincing as he stood.

I scooped an arm under his good shoulder. "We have to get you to the hospital."

"How are we going to explain this? I just killed a cop."

"No. *I* did." My fingerprints were all over the gun now, and I'd rather it have been that way. Michael had done enough with saving my life and all; the least I could do was take the fall for him.

Michael tried to examine Shannon's corpse as we walked

around him to exit the garage gate...no way we were climbing over anything with a bullet hole in my brother. "Well, we better get our story straight before we get there," he said.

He was right, only I had no idea how to explain any of this. No one would believe that Shannon killed Ori and then his brothers, and that after that he tried to kill me and Michael. I touched the spot between my breasts where Shannon had pressed his gun, fingers trembling as they traced a perfectly raised circle. I didn't care what the police thought anymore... Shannon was dead now. Ori could rest peacefully.

CHAPTER THIRTY-THREE

Michael and I had two funerals in as many days and by the time Ori's and Laurel's services were over, I wasn't sure I was ready to go home. I'd bonded with my brother again; we were closer now than we had ever been, and I didn't want my leaving to ruin it. Something in him changed too. His whole personality seemed lighter, like he'd been shackled to a wall in some nasty medieval dungeon for years and had finally been freed.

I stood at my rental car and lit a cigarette, scanning over the people who'd come to say their goodbyes.

"Crazy how many friends she had, huh?" Michael said, walking up to stand beside me. He leaned on the fender, lit a cigarette and leaned his head back to see up into the expanse of oaks branching out above us.

"Yeah, well Laurel knew everybody in this town, so." I flicked my cigarette after taking another drag. My eyes landed on the cluster of police squad cars, feeling somewhat melancholy about Shannon's absence. I was fucked in the head and couldn't help having thoughts that didn't make sense. But my heart couldn't separate its emotions from my brain. My heart still cared for Shannon; I couldn't explain it, and no one needed to know.

"So, you ready to go to the station one last time?" He scratched his freshly shaved cheek, chewed at his thumb nail, fidgeted crossing and uncrossing his feet.

"It's going to be okay, Michael. This is just us signing the final documents of our testimony. They've already cleared us. Stop worrying." I flicked my cigarette to the ground and stepped on it. I bent down to pick it up and he laughed at me.

"Tree hugger." He chuckled.

"Just collecting my DNA." I shoved the butt in my dress pocket and got inside my car, turning over the engine to start it, but it stalled. "What the hell?"

Michael stuck his head inside the open window. "What's the matter?"

"I don't know. It won't start."

He sighed. "Those idiots at that service center mess up all the time. Half our business at the garage was unsatisfied customers from there."

I tried it again, and it was less engaged than the time before. I was carless again. "Guess we are taking your truck," I said, stepping out of my piece of shit and slamming the door shut.

Michael asked if I wanted to listen to the radio, but a headache was thumping the back of my skull, so quiet was good for me. Preemptively, I rolled down the window to avoid getting car sick. My stomach had turned into a wimpy bitch since I arrived in Sweetwater, and I couldn't handle much right now.

We merged onto a two-lane from the cemetery, the speed limit picking up. I leaned my head out the window, the breeze calming my nausea, when I heard the unmistakable sound of a rock stuck in tire treads, click click click on the road. "Pull over a sec," I said, tapping Michael's shoulder.

He slowed, pulled over and watched as I exited the truck. "What are you doing?"

"You've got a rock in your tire. It's driving me crazy."

He shrugged then turned his attention to fetching another smoke.

I walked to the rear tire first, not sure if it was coming from the front or back. When I didn't see anything, I walked up to the front, squatted, and ran my hand over the treads until they hit a hard pebble. I craned my neck to find the stone, a small white one that likely came from the cemetery. I tried to pop it out with my finger, but when that didn't work took a bobby pin from my hair and jabbed it underneath the stone, prying it free. I pinched it between my fingers, realizing immediately it wasn't a stone. I held it to the sky, examining it in better light, and choked on my own gasp as I saw clearly what it was.

A human tooth.

Time froze, my mind went blank, and everything went white, like the end of the fire poker left too long in the coals.

The mix of devastation and the horrific discovery of truth collided, a massive set of hands slapping closed, and the sound rocked my mind awake. Shannon's claim that Ori was hit by a car smacked me harder than Laurel ever had.

I stood up, heart in my throat, and slowly walked back to the car door, sliding in with strangling apprehension.

"Find it?" he asked, jovial.

"Uh...yeah," I managed, a shock of drought in my mouth. I knew Ori had been hit by a car, and now I knew who was driving. My brother.

Ori's brother.

Shannon was right, I needed to look at my own blood. Michael hit Ori with his truck, so why was Shannon covering it up? Nothing made sense. If I said anything right now, he might try to hurt me, or worse. I needed to keep my shit together until we got to the police station, but as we rounded the bend, Michael pulled over again. My heart pounded in my temples, "What's up? You gotta piss?"

I worried I wasn't convincing, hoped like hell the coffee at Laurel's service had worn its welcome.

"What did you find in the tire?" He bothered to stare straight ahead.

"I already told you, a rock...from the funeral."

"Johnna...what did you find in the tire?"

I studied him, saw the purse his lips made when he was cornered. Movement caught my peripheral, and I looked down to see his hand slide underneath his shirt where he kept his gun. "Michael," I whimpered, desperation pulling down the edge of my plea.

"You really don't remember?" he swallowed, a heavy lump sliding down his throat.

"Remember what, Michael?"

"She shouldn't have been in the back of the truck anyway." He chewed the inside of his cheek, tears streaming, a sheen of snot on his upper lip. "God this is so fucked up," he choked.

Tears pooled my eyes. He knew I found something horrible in the tire. "What, Michael? What's fucked up?"

"Ori's graduation night? We were all celebrating?" His stare was a key-twist on a sardine can, as if he could force my brain open to examine it.

"And?"

His nostrils flared. "Goddamnit." He reached for the ignition and yanked the keys. "Here. Take my truck back to D.C. Just leave here and never come back.

"What? No." I swatted the keys away. "Tell me what the fuck happened or so help me God I'm going to that police station and raising more hell than the fucking devil himself!"

"You hit her, Johnna! You were the one driving!"

I wanted to punch him, poke out his eyes, set him on fire. He was a damn liar. "I wasn't even here, Michael."

He nodded, staying silent until he found strength to speak. "That gash in your head," he pointed to the stitched up cut in my hairline. "That's why you don't remember being here. I really thought you'd remember at some point, but..."

I tried to puzzle out his story, but then I remembered, "My agent was with me that weekend. I fell down the stairs in my apartment building and had to go to the hospital. I'd been sleepwalking."

His lips tucked into thin lines as he shook his head. "You didn't fall down any stairs."

I stared at him, waiting for more.

"Call her then. Ask her. She knows."

I didn't have my cell, and there was no way I remembered her number. "Even if that were true...what about Dahlia and Jamie, and—"

"Dahlia was there that night. She wanted us to take Ori to the hospital and when we didn't, she lost her shit. She was going to tell the police on you."

All I could hear was my heart in my ears. "Who killed her?"

"Me."

He said it so quickly that I thought I misheard. "You?" No fucking way he'd do that.

"She would have told the police, and they would have arrested you. I couldn't let that happen."

My chest pounded, nearly stealing my breath. "That's why she was found on the farm?"

He nodded, more tears falling like little confessions leaping off the cliff's ledge. "It wasn't smart, I know, but I wasn't thinking clearly. None of us were."

So Shannon knew Michael killed Dahlia. "Why did Shannon help cover it up?"

He flashed an angry glare at me, eyes red with the horror of it all. "Because he loves you."

I sat quiet for a moment, my mind buzzing, thoughts scattered like marbles out of a broken jar. The visions I'd had of the accident...Ori was still alive, and I knew it. "Why didn't ya'll take her to the hospital?"

"Because I knew Shannon was right. Ori wouldn't have survived; she was almost dead anyway...all those parts everywhere."

I tried not to imagine it, but my mind was quick, and the horror formed anyway. "Kimber killed Jamie, tried to kill me, so Shannon killed him. He was telling the truth this whole time and we killed him for it. And you knew!"

He wiped his hand across his nose.

My vision turned white, anxiety burning my nostrils, acid burning my throat. "Why did you let me think Shannon did it, Michael? Why did you kill him!"

He frowned. "He was the last one to know what really happened. With him gone, it was just a family thing now."

Pressure pushed against my neck as I yelled, and I thought my head would burst. "Laurel knew?"

"Yes." His voice shook and he started taking sharp, shallow breaths, the pitches of air getting faster and louder, spit flying, eyes peeled wide, and then...

His blood splattered everywhere inside the truck. I flinched when fluids and pieces of bone and brain ricocheted off cabin walls and hit me in the face.

I kept my eyes closed for seconds or minutes or hours; I wasn't sure, but the sharp pitch of sirens forced them open. I turned to see out of the back windshield...blue lights, red lights, orange lights, all the colors of the end of the world.

ACKNOWLEDGMENTS

Every story of fiction is born from a spark. If we are lucky, they ignite and burn into fruition. Here's to all the folks who helped douse this book with gasoline.

Thank you to the team at Bloodhound Books. Your guidance and professional care are deeply appreciated. Without you all, this story would still be sitting in a folder on my computer.

Thanks to my AMM Round 3 mentor, Ren Hutchings for teaching me how to elevate my writing. To the Croissant crew for being a light during lockdown; y'all really made those dark times more bearable.

To my frenemy, Chelsea Ichaso, who gave me great feedback on this book and smothered me with kindness and advice.

To my ride or die bitches, Leanne Schwartz and Cate Baumer. You both have been an inspiration beyond words. Thank you for the years of countless encouragement. I can't wait for the day when WE get to have our fancy writing retreat. Oh, the day is coming!

Finally, thank you to my family. You have all supported me, cheered me on, let me wallow in my misery then made me get back up. I can't thank you all enough. Y'all really brought the whole gasoline truck.

ABOUT THE AUTHOR

Heidi Christopher was born in West Virginia, raised in southern North Carolina, and now lives on a mountain in Virginia with her family, which includes a golden retriever, a golden doodle, and four sassy cats. While studying English Literature at Shenandoah University, Heidi was a contributing writer for the University's newspaper. Now, she's a freelance editor specializing in academics for grades K-12. Her debut psychological thriller will be published in November 2025.

You can find out more about Heidi by following her on Instagram @heidicwrites, Bluesky @HeidiChristopher, and X @heidicwrites.

A NOTE FROM THE PUBLISHER

Thank you for reading this book. If you enjoyed it please do consider leaving a review on Amazon to help others find it too.

We hate typos. All of our books have been rigorously edited and proofread, but sometimes mistakes do slip through. If you have spotted a typo, please do let us know and we can get it amended within hours.

info@bloodhoundbooks.com